SEASONS OF
Salvation

SEASONS OF
Salvation

DENNIS L. MANGRUM

CFI
Springville, Utah

ISBN 13: 978-1-55517-949-5
ISBN 10: 1-55517-949-5

Published by CFI, an imprint of Cedar Fort, Inc., 925 N. Main, Springville, UT, 84663
Distributed by Cedar Fort, Inc., www.cedarfort.com

LIBRARY OF CONGRESS CATALOGING-IN-PUBLICATION DATA

    Mangrum, Dennis L.
     Seasons of Salvation / by Dennis L. Mangrum.
       p. cm.
     ISBN-13: 978-1-55517-949-5 (acid-free paper)
     ISBN-10: 1-55517-949-5 (acid-free paper)
     1. Mormons--Fiction. 2. Mormon youth--Fiction. 3. Utah--Fiction. 4. Christmas stories. I. Title.

     PS3613.A537C37 2006
     813'.6--dc22

                       2006015447

Cover design by Nicole Williams
Cover design © 2006 by Lyle Mortimer
Printed in the United States of America

10 9 8 7 6 5 4 3 2

Printed on acid-free paper

Maybe Christmas, he thought, doesn't come from the store.
Maybe Christmas, perhaps, means a little bit more.

—How the Grinch Stole Christmas

Acknowledgments

I must first thank my wife, Liz Mangrum, for the countless times she has gone through the manuscript correcting grammar, punctuation, and word choice. I never got that gene. Without her assistance the story would never have been finished.

Two readers offered insight and suggestions, but more than that, they gave support, hope, and encouragement: my daughter Nichole Jones and my best friend, Laurin Rackham. My son Shane Mangrum, who is infinitely better at writing than I, offered his softly worded criticisms and comments, which in some way also helped smooth the edges of the story. Thanks!

Molonai Hola spun his personal tale at a Christmas party. It so intrigued me that I made him tell his tale to my recorder. From that recording, I formulated the story that became *Seasons of Salvation*. It is based on an event that happened while Molonai was teaching seminary at Granite High School in 1989. Some of the characters are fiction, while others are based on real people.

Preface

I am a witness! I was there, and so in some ways, this is my story. No, that's not right. This is my students' story. I was just along for the ride. This story belongs to them. But to tell it, I have to start way back at the beginning—the beginning of my time—because my grandpa saw it in a dream.

I don't remember many details, but I have been told that I was born in a grass shack on the island of Tonga. They say there was not a doctor around for the delivery. But then, none of my six siblings had a doctor assist them as they made their appearance into this world. It was just my mom and a neighbor lady and eventually me.

I lived a typical Tongan carefree life, never worrying about school or homework or much of anything except having fun in the sun. That all changed abruptly in my eighth year when my grandfather took me aside one Sunday afternoon just before Christmas.

My grandfather was a very respected elder in our village. People whispered that he was very close to the Great Spirit and could see things. He sat me down on the white sands of a blue lagoon. He seemed far away, and I waited for what seemed like a long while for him to speak.

He told me that my mother and father were going to take my family and me to America, to a place called Utah. He said it was in the United States. "Where is that?" I asked. "Can you get there by canoe?"

He laughed and told me no, that it would not be anything like Tonga and that he had been told that it snowed in Utah at Christmastime. I asked, "Snow?"

"Yes, snow. It falls from the sky like rain but is cold and white," he said as he gestured with his hands. He told me he had never seen it but that it was white and beautiful.

I asked my grandfather why we were leaving the island to go to this place so far away, so full of snow. "Because," he said, "you need an education. There are people out there," he motioned across the water, "that only you can help. Spirits are waiting for you. You will be a leader—someone to follow."

"Why?" I asked him.

He paused and said that he had dreamed a dream. He had seen me in his dream at a place called a university, where many students came to learn. He told me that many people would look to me for guidance. I would become a leader and make a difference in people's lives.

"When will I get to come home?"

He looked at me with a fierceness that belied his age and said, "Jacob Wolfgramm, I don't think you will ever return to live in this place. This is not your place. Our Father has other plans for you in that faraway land. Remember, there are things that only you can do, people that you must touch. But remember us always and never forget."

"When will I see you again, Grandpa?" I asked.

"Though you will be far way, I will always be with you in spirit. But I don't think I'll see you again on this side of the veil."

My grandfather was wise, and I knew he saw truth. It's hard for me to remember his words, but I will never forget the feeling

I had when he spoke them—not ever. It seems at times that my grandfather is still near—especially at Christmas.

Robert Forester, director of the Granite High School church seminary program, stood up from his desk and warmly shook Jacob Wolfgramm's hand.

"Welcome, Jacob," he said. Instead of returning to sit behind his desk, Brother Forester pulled up two chairs facing each other in front of the desk.

"Sit down," he said. "It was good of you to come. I've missed having our little talks."

Jacob grimaced and then chuckled. "Talks? Is that what you call them?"

"So, Jake, how is our star football player doing at the University of Utah this year?"

Jacob burst out laughing. He laughed a lot. "I don't think anyone but you calls me a star. In fact, my coach has a few other names for me."

"Sounds like you've suddenly developed a serious case of humility, Jake," Brother Forester joked. "We'll see how long that lasts. Anyway, tell me about your girlfriend. Tell me how you're doing."

"No girlfriend. I don't have time. Besides, I haven't found one that will go out with me. As for my life, well, you see, the football coach believes the only reason we are at the university is to play football. We practice about five hours a day, six days a week. At the end of practice, all I want to do is crawl into bed. And you know that myth about teachers giving football players a break? Well it just ain't true!"

Brother Forester was proud of Jake. He beamed with delight for the success of his former student. Jacob Wolfgramm was someone unique: a struggling student, a starter on the football team, president of the 28,000 students at the University of Utah, and humble on top of it all—well, kind of humble.

Jacob's thoughts flashed back to his life seven years before when he was a sophomore at Granite High School. He had been headed the wrong way down a one-way street. With English skills that were lacking and schooling at the bottom of his to-do list, he was the leader of a gang on a collision course with trouble.

Fortunately, Jacob ran into a roadblock named Brother Forester. Brother Forester had been Jacob's religion teacher in a seminary program sponsored by the Mormon Church. Seminary was offered to students who wanted to take a religion class during high school. Those students could obtain release time during the day to attend seminary classes off campus.

Brother Forester forcefully pushed his way into Jacob's life. One day he saw Jacob taking lunch money from kids, telling them it was "protection money." Jacob guaranteed that no one would hurt them as long as he got money. Instead of dragging Jake to the school administration, Brother Forester dragged him into his office to have what he called a "little talk."

"Jake, I've been watching you," said Brother Forester. Jake knew he was in trouble. This wasn't the first time he had confiscated lunch money from fellow students.

Brother Forester threw a sucker punch of sorts at Jacob, catching him completely off guard. He asked, "Do you believe that you can be president of Granite High School?"

"Are you nuts?" responded Jake. "Why would I want to be

president of this high school? Besides, no one would vote for me unless I beat them up."

Brother Forester looked at Jacob for some time as if he were sizing him up. "Because, Jake, Granite High needs you even if you don't need it. You are a born leader, and people love to follow you. You can make this a better school. I believe in you, Jake. I believe you can rise above the image of a Polynesian dropout. I believe you can be an example to everyone. You are a mold breaker." With that he just stared at Jake.

Jake looked at Brother Forester. "You're serious, aren't you?"

"Never been more serious, Jake. This school needs you."

Jake left Brother Forester's office promising he would discontinue his student-protection business. He thought a lot about what Brother Forester had said and had trouble sleeping that night. At one point he must have been dozing because he sat straight up and tried to remember his dream. Then he heard the voice. It was his grandfather talking to him when he had left Tonga.

"Jacob," he had said, "you are going to America to get an education because you have people to help. You will be someone to follow—a leader."

So that made at least two people telling him that he was a leader. What did they know?

The next morning, Jake found Brother Forester in his office. He sat down in a chair and asked, "Okay, how do I do it?" The meeting that day was the first of many. Brother Forester would teach and Jake would listen, and Jake would ask questions and Brother Forester would respond. Brother Forester cared. He was willing to invest his time and energy into Jake.

During one talk, Brother Forester asked, "Jake, have you ever dreamed dreams of what you want to be?"

Jake thoughtfully responded, "No, but my grandfather did. I just thought I would pour concrete and maybe build a few houses with my father."

"Your grandfather dreamed what?" asked Brother Forester.

"In the Tongan culture," Jacob replied, "it seems that every family has a dreamer. Dreamers enjoy an elite status among my people. Anyway," he continued, "before I left Tonga, my grandfather told me he had dreamed of me and some of the things I would do in America. You know, it's not strange for people to dream in the islands—I mean dream dreams of what may happen. I guess it's like seeing into the future. In our family it was my grandfather. In Tonga the people believe in these dreams. Me? I don't know, but I doubt that anyone can see things that are yet to happen."

Jake was suddenly silent, staring nowhere. "Jake," Brother Forester said after a minute, "Jake, are you still with me?"

"Oh, sorry. I was just thinking. The other night it was like my grandfather was right here talking to me. I don't remember a lot about the islands, but I do remember my grandfather."

Brother Forester often talked to Jake about his grandfather and the dreams. It was clear that Brother Forester believed in dreams. Jake continued to express his reservations, although he wasn't sure why.

That year Jacob was elected president of his high school. After receiving the election results, he found Brother Forester sitting in his office. The mentor was grinning when Jake walked in. "From gangster to president in three short years," Brother Forester laughed. "Congratulations, Jake, I knew you had it in you."

"Yeah, you and my grandfather," Jake mumbled. After the two friends had talked for some time, Jake finally said, "You know, none of this would have been possible without you, Brother Forester. Why did you pick on me?"

"It wasn't me, Jake. I just did as I was told," replied Brother Forester.

"No, Brother Forester, it was you. You could have just turned me in to the administration and I would have been out of school, but you didn't. You cared enough to talk to me, to direct me, to lead me. You spent hundreds of hours with me. There aren't many people like you in the world, Brother Forester. I owe you big time."

"Jake, you don't owe me anything. Just watching you succeed is all the thanks I will ever need. One day when you're rich and famous, I'll call in the debt."

Jacob's thoughts returned to the present. He wondered if Brother Forester could now be calling in the debt. It was apparent that Brother Forester was still talking to him and had not noticed that Jake was somewhere else for a while.

"Jake," Brother Forester said, looking straight at him, "I have a favor to ask. Now, you need to hear me out before you say no!"

"Are you calling in the debt, Brother Forester?" asked Jake.

"And what debt would that be?"

"You remember. The day I was elected student body president and I told you I owed you big time."

"Yeah, you could say I'm calling in the debt. Jake, I know how busy you are with school and all. But we need you. The Lord needs you, busy or not."

"All you have to do is ask," Jacob replied.

"Let me lay my cards on the table," Brother Forester began. "I have this seminary class that starts at 6 A.M. every day. And yes, that's in the morning. I do remember how you like mornings. The class will be filled with kids who have been kicked out of their regular classes because they have behavioral problems. Some of the kids will come to class because their parents make them, and others—who knows? But almost all of the kids are misfits in one way or another. You know the kind," he finished, winking.

"Yeah, sounds like you're talkin' about me, Brother Forester," Jacob replied, nodding thoughtfully.

"I didn't say that," said Brother Forester. "But then you might be able to relate to some of these kids in a way that others can't. Anyway, I don't have a teacher for the class, and I need someone who understands these kids—someone who talks the talk and can't be physically intimidated by them. Someone who isn't afraid to sit a problem kid down and explain it so that he understands. Mostly I need someone who cares about kids, kids that everyone else has given up on. In short, I need you."

"Brother Forester, you know I'd do anything for you. But

teach a class every morning? I just don't know!"

"Jake, I don't know how you will find the time, but I promise that if you take the job, you will never regret your decision." He paused for a minute and then added, "Oh yeah, I forgot to tell you about the pay. It's a volunteer position. But at least you will be putting the Lord in your debt for a change."

Jacob looked as if he didn't feel well.

"Before you answer," Brother Forester asked, "do you understand what it is I'm asking you to do?"

"I think so," Jacob answered.

"No, Jake, I don't think you do," Brother Forester cautioned. "You see, this early morning class is a bunch of real characters who don't fit in anywhere. These kids don't want to be in school, let alone seminary at 6 in the morning.

"There are a few students in the class who are taking early morning seminary because they have too many other classes to take during the day. But for the most part, these kids will push you to the limit in every direction you can imagine. I could tell you that we have teachers lining up to take this class, but that wouldn't be true. Fact is, I can't get anyone to take on this group of kids. And these are the kids who need it more than anyone else. They all need you, Jake.

"Oh, and one more thing. Classes start in less than three weeks, so you might want to start looking at the first few lessons. Your manual is in the chair next to you."

Jake appeared lost. "So I assume you knew I would accept."

"Jake, I really hate to do this to you, but then maybe you deserve it. Maybe it was something bad you did when you were a kid. Call me if you need any help with the lessons."

Chapter 1
AUGUST 1

Cheyenne Carson watched the judge and recalled the countless times she'd been in this exact seat. She felt tired of this game she was expected to play—one more foster home, one more rejection, one more round of "Mother May I?"

She glanced at Mrs. Lloyd. *Crazy lady*, she thought, though deep down, she felt a little satisfaction that someone wanted her.

She knew it wouldn't last, though, and even Mrs. Lloyd would get tired of playing house. In Cheyenne's experience, life didn't happen like it did in the movies or how you wanted it to. She sat in the witness chair in the court of Judge Stephen Wentworth.

Richard and Nichole Lloyd sat at one counsel table while the director of the Division of Family Services sat at the other. Today they would learn if the judge would award the Lloyds legal custody of Cheyenne.

Cheyenne was anxious and had mixed feelings. It felt weird that she was finally being adopted. So many foster homes and foster parents had come and gone in her life, and most of them she wanted to forget. Most had been temporary stopping places that had not worked for her or for the foster parents. She was the problem—at least that's what everyone said. It seemed to her that no one, including her social workers and counselors, ever really cared to hear her side of the story.

She wondered why the Lloyds were seeking to adopt her. At seventeen, she was not a hot commodity in the adoption market. She had never felt like a hot commodity in any market, for that matter.

She inwardly grimaced but clung to the defiant thought, *It doesn't really matter anyway.* She knew that no matter what happened today, as soon as she turned eighteen, which was in a few months, she would be free to do whatever she wanted, and never again would anyone be able to tell her what to do.

Still, the Lloyds wanted to adopt her.

There were no financial benefits in adoptions like the benefits foster parents received. There was not a trial period to see if you fit in the family. The Lloyds would become her parents, like it or not, and she would become their child, like it or not.

Why would they want to adopt me? she mused. Things just didn't add up. Only once had she spoken with Mrs. Lloyd, and she had never talked with Mr. Lloyd. Where did any of this come from? Why hadn't there been interviews? And how did Mrs. Lloyd know so much about her life?

Cheyenne had to hide a smile as Mrs. Lloyd told the court that she didn't need Family Services, or anyone else for that matter, informing her about adoption or the consequences of bringing a teenager into her home. Judge Wentworth was not pleased by her tone, and yet he seemed to enjoy her no-nonsense position. Cheyenne wondered why the judge put up with Mrs. Lloyd. She knew where she would be if she argued with the judge, and it wouldn't be walking in the park.

Mrs. Lloyd continued to argue with the judge. Cheyenne watched quietly, drifting off into her own world. *Home,* she thought. People tossed around that term so loosely. In seventeen years, she had never lived in a place she could call home. She had been bounced around among foster houses, agency houses, and even detention centers. She knew one thing for sure—none of them had been a home to her. Her real father and mother were a mystery. She didn't even know their names. Apparently, her mother didn't even know her father's name.

What had she done to be left so alone? At the age of one, the police had discovered her behind a 7-Eleven store wrapped in a blanket held together with a braided rope. A note pinned to the blanket read:

"I cannot take care of my daughter any longer. I don't know her father, and I don't have any hope. Maybe someone can give her the things I would never be able to provide. Her name is Cheyenne. I once passed through there. I have always thought that her last name should be Carson. It was always my favorite name. I'm sorry I couldn't give her more. She is such a sweet baby. I think she is beautiful."

So she became Cheyenne Carson. At least that's what her birth certificate issued by Salt Lake County stated. Under "father" and "mother," one simple and yet vague word was printed: "Unknown." She wasn't just an orphan. She had no one. Everyone had left her. Cheyenne wondered how different her life would have been had she had a mother. She used to dream when she was little of a real mother—someone who would hold her when she felt sad, someone who would dry her tears when she cried, someone who would really listen and try to understand her feelings. Such dreams had ended a long, long time ago. Besides, they were just dreams, and there are no fairy tales in real life.

She had been asked to leave more than one foster house. By the time she had reached age eight, she had lived in two orphanages, several group homes, and six different foster houses. None had ever felt like *home.* The reports described her in less than favorable terms: "Cheyenne believes there is one way to do things, and that's her way." "She is obviously very clever, but she is also withdrawn, almost sullen, and doesn't display affection toward anyone." "She doesn't get along with other children in the family." And finally, "She doesn't like anyone."

On and on the complaint lists went, with no space on the

forms for Cheyenne's comments. She couldn't remember being asked to explain from her point of view why things did not work out. She could have told them about spoiled brats, unfair treatment, and ugly sisters. In her mind, even Cinderella had had it better than she did. At least Cinderella had secret helpers who took her to the ball. Cheyenne just got taken to the agency house, and there were no balls or glass slippers waiting for her there.

She knew no one wanted to listen. She had learned the hard way that it was easier to keep out of sight, out of mind. She never drew attention to herself; never let them know she was smart, and never cared about anyone because they would leave, just like her mother did. To Cheyenne, relationships were always temporary.

She thought back to the time she had spent with the Schmidt family. She was almost twelve when she was placed in their home. They were getting paid for having a foster child. They needed the money and used it to pay the mortgage. They didn't care about her.

Cheyenne slept in the unfinished basement. In six months, the Schmidts had never given her any clothes, not even hand-me-downs. She had only the clothes she brought with her. The social workers never had a clue.

At twelve Cheyenne didn't understand much, but she knew she had to leave, so she decided to run. She was only twelve, but she already felt old.

She remembered Disneyland photos she had seen and decided to go there. She took $70 from Mrs. Schmidt's purse and headed out. She even found the bus depot, but her plan was foiled when she tried to buy a ticket to Disneyland. Back she went to Youth Services. From that point on, whenever someone was missing money, she got the blame.

The director of Family Services was reading from a report. It recommended against granting adoption at this time. Time was needed for the Lloyds and the minor to evaluate the relationship.

"Granting an adoption at this point," the report read, "would be like jumping off a cliff without knowing what was below."

The Lloyds' attorney objected, but his objection was overruled.

Mrs. Lloyd stood to say something, but her husband grabbed her arm and pulled her into her seat. "You're in enough trouble," he whispered. "Don't add to it. Let our attorney talk for a minute."

Cheyenne had learned that she couldn't ever win a fight with a judge or anyone in authority. She had learned to stay in the shadows. Out of harm's way. But she liked Mrs. Lloyd's spunk. She was a fighter who didn't hide in the shadows. It almost made her laugh. But then she wondered if she could live in the same house with someone who was so bossy. This lady was a tiger, but then maybe the judge had just backed her into a corner.

The one thing that especially caught Cheyenne's attention was that Mrs. Lloyd wouldn't let anyone say anything bad about her. She had an answer for everything. She was almost like a bear guarding her cubs, and it occurred to Cheyenne that maybe Mrs. Lloyd really did want to adopt her. But Cheyenne couldn't think of why.

What does she know about me? Why does she care about me? Mrs. Lloyd sure didn't look like any foster parent she had ever seen. She was very pretty, young, and full of life. She had a sparkle in her eye. She was intriguing. Cheyenne reminded herself that she didn't have anything to lose. Only six or eight months. And besides, what was her second choice?

At seventeen, Cheyenne looked street tough. She was no more than 110 pounds and stood five feet nine inches. She had purposely dyed her honey-colored hair jet-black, leaving the lighter roots showing. A black shirt and black pants completed her look.

She tried to live in the shadows. She avoided recognition and attention. She survived.

The judge asked Mrs. Lloyd a series of questions. "Have you read this girl's complete file? Do you know how many foster homes she has been in? Do you know that she has a history of stealing? Do you know how many times she has run from a foster home? Have you read the psychologist reports?"

Cheyenne could have responded to the questions, but, as usual, no one asked her. Everyone always told her what she was going to do, where she was going to live, and how she was supposed to act. She knew exactly where she stood in the pecking order, and it wasn't at the top of any list.

Mrs. Lloyd's steel-blue eyes seemed to bore right through Cheyenne. She felt them every time Mrs. Lloyd looked in her direction. They seemed to see inside her and yet radiated kindness.

Mrs. Lloyd had been quiet after Judge Wentworth's questions, but then she gave him a look that said, "Do you think I'm stupid?" She politely but resolutely responded, "Yes! I've read every single word of those files. *Have you?*"

The judge looked questioningly at Mrs. Lloyd and responded with equal intensity, "Then tell me one good reason that you want to take this young woman into your home. If you have indeed read the reports, then you know that every other family that has given her a chance has failed. What makes you think you will fare any better?"

Mrs. Lloyd turned to look at Cheyenne. It was not just a glance, it was a soul-searching stare, intense and yet warm and inviting. Cheyenne could not release Mrs. Lloyd's eyes. She seemed to be trying to say something to her without speaking. Finally, Mrs. Lloyd turned her attention to the judge and quietly asked, "Have you ever seen a lily before it unfolds, before the light awakens it?" She paused, turned back to look at Cheyenne for emphasis, and with conviction said, "Besides, someone that I care very much about once told me that you don't throw a life away just because it's broken a little."

Cheyenne wasn't sure why, but she was suddenly filled with a feeling of peace, a warm feeling of caring and comfort, and then, just as suddenly, it was gone. It was the same feeling she had in her room at the detention center, a room without windows and only bars for a door. She could remember looking at a

Bible and thinking, *God? No, there wasn't a God! Not around here.*
She had never allowed herself to consider the possibility, yet she
found herself leafing through the pages of the small, black leather
book. She stopped at a verse someone had marked in red. It was
Matthew 6:28–30, 32, from the Sermon on the Mount. It read:

"Why take ye thought for raiment? Consider the lilies of the
field, how they grow; they toil not, neither do they spin: and yet
I say unto you that even Solomon in all his glory was not arrayed
like one of these. Wherefore, if God so clothe the grass of the
field, which to day is, and to morrow is cast into the oven, shall
he not much more clothe you, O ye of little faith? . . . For your
Heavenly Father knoweth that ye have need of all these things."

The verse had for some reason struck a chord in her heart.
She hadn't heard any words or seen a vision, but she had felt a
calm peace flood through her soul, a peace growing from the
inside out. She had never experienced such a feeling, but then it
was gone just as quickly as it had come. She knew she had felt
something real because she now felt the loss of it.

Cheyenne had tried to rekindle the feeling. She read the verse
again and again. Nothing, yet she knew she had felt something.
The void amplified her memory of that fleeting feeling and made
an indefinable impact on her heart.

That night she had sat on her bed and thought for a long
time. The verse almost seemed to be asking her a direct question.
She did not have to worry about her clothes, a home, or even a
mother and father because God, if there was such a person, knew
that she needed those things.

"I suppose, then, that God doesn't think I need a mother or a
father," she'd said to herself. Then she laughed at the thought.

Cheyenne looked again at the defiant lady sitting at the
counsel table. She was different from all of the other do-gooders.
Cheyenne knew it. She felt it. And then Cheyenne caught herself
and remembered that relationships never last. *Don't get caught in
that trap,* she reminded herself.

The director of Family Services thought Mrs. Lloyd just
didn't understand. He thought that she didn't have a clue about

teenagers or was just plain naive. Standing, he haughtily replied to Mrs. Lloyd's unsophisticated response, "And I suppose you know this because of female intuition? Or do you have some rationale upon which to base your suppositions?"

Cheyenne wondered why Mrs. Lloyd was willing to wage war against the world for her. Whatever the reason, it didn't seem that Mrs. Lloyd was about to let anyone, including a judge, some stuffy civil servant, or anyone else get in her way. She was definitely spunky.

Suddenly the judge got everyone's attention. He rapped his gavel on his bench three times, and then he spoke. This time Cheyenne felt that he was speaking directly to her, although he was addressing his comments to Mrs. Lloyd.

"Mrs. Lloyd, in several months, Miss Carson will turn eighteen. After she turns eighteen, she will not be treated as a juvenile but as an adult. She needs to start acting like one." Then his tone became more conciliatory. "I have seen a lot of girls like Miss Carson come through these doors. Most go on to live a life that I don't think you can even begin to imagine. I wish it were not so. I wish there were a magic wand I could wave to help these girls. But it doesn't work that way. I strongly advise you against continuing your quest for adoption."

Mrs. Lloyd would not be swayed. She was tough. "Thank you, your Honor, for your advice and recommendations. I have listened and considered carefully all you have said. Also, I have considered all of the reports in Miss Carson's file as well as spoken with some of her counselors. My husband and I still very much want to adopt Miss Carson. It's the right thing for us to do, and it's right for Cheyenne."

Judge Wentworth was not impressed. He turned his attention toward Richard Lloyd.

"Mr. Lloyd, you have been very quiet during these proceedings. Do you concur with your wife's decision?"

Mr. Lloyd stood, glanced at his wife, and then looked at Cheyenne. Then with a smile, he turned toward the judge and spoke. "Your Honor, I only get one vote in my family and that won't carry the house." Mrs. Lloyd smirked while Mr. Lloyd laughed to himself.

Mr. Lloyd continued, "Seriously, though, we would be honored to have Miss Carson share our home with us. It's like my wife said, 'It's the right thing.'" With that, he looked at Cheyenne in a way that let her know he meant what he said. He reached over, gave his wife a hug, and sat down.

Cheyenne didn't know how to interpret the many feelings flooding over her, but she knew these two people were unlike any others she had known as foster parents.

Judge Wentworth responded. He was intimidating and his concern was not directed to the Lloyds but to Cheyenne. He was not happy. "Mr. and Mrs. Lloyd, I am going to grant you temporary custody of Miss Carson as of this date. However, I am going to reserve the issue of final adoption for further proceedings at a time to be determined. Let's call it a trial period. Mrs. Lloyd, you are going to have to make a personal appearance before me every two weeks to report on Miss Carson's progress. However, don't mistake my meaning. If she has any problems, she will go to Decker Lake, the juvenile center, until she is eighteen. Do you understand?"

The Lloyds both nodded their understanding. But it wasn't a conciliatory nod, not from Mrs. Lloyd; it was an in-your-face acceptance without any acquiescence.

The judge then turned to face Cheyenne. "Young lady, have you been listening to me?" She didn't speak, but she nodded. "Well, this is your last chance, and if I hear that you have caused Mr. or Mrs. Lloyd any grief, you will not receive any mercy from this court. Further, young lady, you are to immediately start school and you are not to miss one day without a medical excuse that is signed by a doctor. Do you understand me?"

Cheyenne again nodded her head without looking into the judge's eyes. Defiance burned inside, but she didn't want the judge to notice it. She responded quietly and with controlled anger, "I understand."

Judge Wentworth directed the bailiff to release her to the

Lloyds' care. With that, the judge hit the gavel and dismissed the court.

Once again, Cheyenne was being told what to do. But the Lloyds were different. Would this be just another short layover on her path to . . . to . . . She wished she knew where all of this would end.

Chapter 2

AUGUST 26

Cheyenne was lying on "her bed" in "her room" in a house she had been told was "her home." At least that's what Mrs. Lloyd had called it. Cheyenne wasn't sure how she felt about all this "her" stuff, but she did know that the Lloyds had made her feel like she belonged. She was comfortable in the Lloyd house. She thought back over the past three weeks. A lot had changed in her life in a very short time, and it all seemed for the better.

She tried to caution herself, however. Relationships for her had always been temporary. Mrs. Lloyd had been very nice to her. But Cheyenne knew even *nice* ended. She was not about to start caring for someone only to have her gone later. She vowed to herself again that she would be polite yet reserved, wary, and prepared for anything.

Prepared or not, Cheyenne knew she had been caught in Mrs. Lloyd's web. She couldn't help but like her. Mrs. Lloyd had a way of making everyone feel at ease. Every time Cheyenne called her Mrs. Lloyd, she would shake her head and say, "I want you to call me Nichole, not ma'am or Mrs. Lloyd. Mrs. Lloyd makes me sound like an old lady, and ma'am sounds like I belong in . . . well, *Gone with the Wind,* or something very old or formal. I don't fit any of those categories. And if I do, then you'd better not tell me."

It always made Cheyenne smile just a little. *Spunky, definitely spunky,* she thought.

Cheyenne knew Mrs. Lloyd was bending over backward to treat her with respect. She knew Mrs. Lloyd wanted her to feel comfortable in her home. The Lloyds were still trying to adopt her. Mrs. Lloyd didn't have any ulterior motives that Cheyenne could discover, but she could not bring herself to trust Mrs. Lloyd or to believe the situation was anything more than temporary.

And yet, Cheyenne wanted to believe that this might work. She had always yearned for a mother or a friend, and here was Mrs. Lloyd offering both to her on a silver platter. Cheyenne wanted nothing more than to be able to talk to someone who cared about her, about what she thought. She didn't want to have to be guarded about everything she said. So Cheyenne struggled, caught between hope and reality.

Just yesterday Cheyenne woke up to the aroma of bacon, eggs, and pancakes. When she walked out of the bedroom, Mrs. Lloyd said, "Good morning, Cheyenne. Sit down. I just made a little something for us to eat."

Cheyenne felt awkward and replied, "A little something? It looks like a feast. You don't have to cook breakfast for me."

"No, I don't, but I've always wanted to spoil someone. And since there isn't anyone else around but you and Richard, I guess it will have to be you. Besides, if I spoil Richard any more, he might start thinking he's entitled to it."

Cheyenne tried to explain. "I . . . know but . . . but no one's ever . . . well, thank you, but . . . oh well . . . thank you, Mrs. Lloyd."

Mrs. Lloyd let out an impatient moan, "I thought I told you . . ."

"All right, all right. I'm trying . . . Nichole."

"Now that wasn't so hard, was it?" asked Mrs. Lloyd.

The problem was that Cheyenne realized that she was

beginning to like Mrs. Lloyd. That was another warning flag. She couldn't get trapped into caring.

Cheyenne remembered vividly the day Mrs. Lloyd took her to see her high school counselor, Mrs. Miller, who had told Mrs. Lloyd, "We can't tell you if she can graduate this year until we have contacted every school she has attended to get her credits."

Mrs. Lloyd answered, "Let's start calling. There is no time like the present. Besides, we only have to speak to those where she has taken high school classes. And if you are too busy, just tell me what to do and I'll do it, but I'm not leaving here today until we find out just where she stands."

Mrs. Lloyd had gone to bat for Cheyenne. Why? Cheyenne knew that ensuring high school graduation didn't fit into the job description of a foster parent.

Cheyenne could remember her last court appearance before Judge Wentworth. She smiled as she remembered leaving the courthouse with Mrs. Lloyd. Mrs. Lloyd had told her husband after leaving the courthouse, "Don't worry about me and Cheyenne. Go back to work. I have a few things planned for us to do. Girl things, okay?"

Mrs. Lloyd didn't explain to Cheyenne what the "girl things" were. She simply led Cheyenne to her car and drove away without saying anything. Cheyenne wondered, *girl things?* She continued to wonder until Mrs. Lloyd stopped the car in a parking lot outside the Cottonwood Mall. Mrs. Lloyd carefully looked Cheyenne over from head to foot as she got out of the car. Cheyenne felt embarrassed. Mrs. Lloyd tilted her head to one side and said, "I think I know how to fix the problem. You need some clothes. How about we go shopping and then get something very chocolaty to eat? Okay?"

Cheyenne was surprised and didn't know quite what to say. She finally stammered, "I . . . I don't think . . . I don't have any money."

Mrs. Lloyd scrunched her nose up and said, "Well, that could be a problem, but I do have Richard's credit card. And everyone around my house gets new clothes for school. So the treat's on me, or maybe Richard. But let's not tell him about the card right now, okay?" Then she laughed and said, "Just kidding, it's my credit card."

As they walked into the mall, Mrs. Lloyd continued to carry on a one-sided conversation. "So, Cheyenne, where should we start?"

Cheyenne was perplexed. Mrs. Lloyd had an ability to always keep her off balance. "I guess we could try The Express," Cheyenne mumbled. She knew this was not the type of store Mrs. Lloyd would frequent, but Mrs. Lloyd didn't object. Cheyenne couldn't help but wonder how long Mrs. Lloyd would play this "being nice" game.

Cheyenne picked out some clothes because Mrs. Lloyd wouldn't let her say no. They looked similar to the dark ones she was wearing, but they were new. Then Mrs. Lloyd made her pick out some personal items, socks, and even a couple pair of shoes. Cheyenne wondered why Mrs. Lloyd was treating her so kindly. Nobody took her shopping. What did she want from Cheyenne? Whatever it was, Mrs. Lloyd was out of luck because Cheyenne didn't have it.

She knew Mrs. Lloyd had not approved of her choice in clothes, but Mrs. Lloyd had not said a single negative word and had signed on the dotted line to pay for them all.

Then out of the blue, Mrs. Lloyd said, "I think I need some chocolate. Right now. Don't you agree?" They strolled to the food court, and Mrs. Lloyd ordered a double chocolate malt with a large order of french fries. "Your turn to order, Cheyenne. Go ahead and splurge. We owe it to ourselves. You don't get any of my fries, so you'd better get your own."

Cheyenne tried not to smile. "I'll take a cheeseburger and a Coke, okay?" and looked at Mrs. Lloyd for approval.

"You'd better give her an order of fries too. I know she'll want some of mine."

Mrs. Lloyd was a talking machine. She wasn't the least bit shy about telling Cheyenne personal things. She told her she was twenty-one when she met Richard and how they had fallen in love. Then she asked, as if Cheyenne were her closest friend, "How about you, Cheyenne? Have you ever been in love?"

Cheyenne was taken aback. No one had ever asked her such a personal question before. No one had ever cared about her life. She responded meekly and hesitantly, "No . . . no . . . me and boys . . . no, no."

Mrs. Lloyd didn't push it any further but went right on talking until she finished her lunch. Then she announced, "Well, we have one more stop to make. Let's walk over to Meier and Frank, okay?"

Mrs. Lloyd went straight to the newest fashions. She sorted through all kinds of clothes. Cheyenne patiently watched as Mrs. Lloyd eyed the clothes. Occasionally she would look at Cheyenne and then go back to the clothes. She picked out three complete outfits: one formal, one casual, and one to wear to church. Then she said to Cheyenne, "Go try these on for me, will you? I want to see how each of them fits. Model them for me just like they do on the runway. I'll wait right here."

"Why don't you try them on yourself?" asked Cheyenne.

"I want to see how they look on you, okay?" replied Mrs. Lloyd.

Cheyenne put on the first outfit and walked out of the dressing room. She tried to look dignified and even struck a few modeling poses. Mrs. Lloyd laughed and said, "You look drop-dead gorgeous in that outfit, Cheyenne. It's a good thing there aren't any boys around here."

One by one Cheyenne tried on the outfits, and Mrs. Lloyd always had something nice to say about the way she looked. Cheyenne wasn't used to having someone tell her she looked nice, and she didn't quite know how to react. The clothes? Well, Cheyenne thought they would look nice on someone else, someone who wanted to be noticed.

"So how do you like them?" asked Mrs. Lloyd.

"You'll look really nice in them, Mrs. Lloyd. You'll be hot."

"But I'm not buying them for me," replied Mrs. Lloyd. "They are yours."

"But . . . I . . . they just aren't . . ."

"Not to worry, Cheyenne. The day may come when you may need them. Maybe not right now, but one day. Humor me, okay?" That was it, and Cheyenne walked out with three new outfits that were definitely not her style.

When they arrived home that day, Mrs. Lloyd took Cheyenne into a cozy, little bedroom in the basement of the Lloyds' new split-level home. She told Cheyenne, "This will be your own room, Cheyenne, and this will be your home. I expect that you will treat it with respect. I want you to keep your room clean. Most of all, Cheyenne, I want you to know that you will be loved in this home. We will expect certain things from you, and we will do all we can to help you. We will not tolerate dishonesty or laziness. But most of all, we want you to know that you can call this place home for as long as you want. You will not be sent away from here unless you choose to go or break our trust."

Mrs. Lloyd hung the new clothes in Cheyenne's closet. "Dinner will be at 6:30, okay? Please feel free to explore. If you have any questions or just want to talk, I'll be around."

The shopping expedition had been three weeks ago, although it seemed like it had been longer. Cheyenne had loved every minute of those three weeks. She was living a dream. She had been treated with respect, given chores, and asked to help Mrs. Lloyd from time to time. Mrs. Lloyd had a great library, and Cheyenne was able to read anything she wanted. Every day Mrs. Lloyd had things planned for them to do. "Girl things," she called them. While they worked, they talked. It had become easier to talk to Mrs. Lloyd. Cheyenne had found a friend. She also came to understand that school was not a "have to," it was a "get to" in the Lloyd home. Cheyenne was expected to be a serious student. Mrs. Lloyd said she would be available to help her with any homework or school problems.

No one had ever been involved in Cheyenne's personal life. And for that matter, no one had ever cared. Good grades drew attention, and she had learned to avoid any attention. But that didn't seem like a plan that would fly at the Lloyd home. Mrs. Lloyd had said, "You know, Cheyenne, I get this sneaking feeling that you could be a very good student if you wanted."

"Now what would give you that idea?" Cheyenne asked.

"Well, nothing except that your test scores appear to be off the charts while your grades are always just passing."

Cheyenne wasn't about to get into that discussion so she asked, "It seems that you guys take this religion thing pretty seriously."

It seemed that religion flowed in and out of any conversation with Mrs. Lloyd. Not that she was pushy, but Mrs. Lloyd was definitely religious. "Cheyenne, I know we kind of squeezed you into religion," she said. "I hope you are not offended. I just wanted you to understand just what it is that we believe in this home."

"Don't worry about it, Mrs. . . . . I mean Nichole. It's always interested me how some people can actually believe God exists. I've never seen him in my neighborhood. There was one time . . . I had this feeling . . . but, it wasn't anything."

Mrs. Lloyd did not push too hard that day. However, Cheyenne learned that the basic tenets of Mrs. Lloyd's religion centered on being the best person she could be to everyone.

During one of their talks, Mrs. Lloyd had explained how important families were to her. She had explained that she believed "families can be forever," that special relationships did not end with death but continued throughout the eternities.

Without thinking, Cheyenne asked, "If you love families so much, how come you don't have any children?" Cheyenne shocked herself with the question.

Mrs. Lloyd suddenly became very quiet, so unlike herself, and responded softly, "One day I'll tell you a story, Cheyenne, but not today. All in good time." And that was it. Cheyenne wondered what Mrs. Lloyd was avoiding, but she did not dare to ask.

A knock sounded on Cheyenne's bedroom door. It was Mrs. Lloyd, who always afforded Cheyenne the courtesy of a knock. Cheyenne had never been in a home where her foster parents knocked on her door. They usually just charged in, hoping to catch her doing something wrong. Mrs. Lloyd, however, knocked and waited until she was invited in.

Mrs. Lloyd appeared to be very nervous, which again was strange for her. She came in and sat on the bed across from Cheyenne, wringing her hands and not looking at Cheyenne. Finally she said, "I need to talk to you, Cheyenne." She sounded unsure, hesitant. At that moment, Mrs. Lloyd wasn't the same confident person Cheyenne had come to know. Cheyenne felt her throat go dry, dreading what was coming.

"Cheyenne, I know you haven't known me long. I guess you wonder why we want to adopt you. I don't know what or how you feel about it. I know I have to consider your feelings and I've wondered. I've wanted to talk to you. I just don't know where to start."

Cheyenne was confused. She had no idea what Mrs. Lloyd was talking about or why she was nervous. Was she going to ask Cheyenne to leave? Send her back to a family care center? Cheyenne felt her stomach tie into a large lump. She didn't know what to say. She knew everything was only temporary. She knew that all of this had been too good to be true. *Oh well, at least Judge Wentworth couldn't blame this one on her,* she thought.

Finally Mrs. Lloyd just blurted out, "Cheyenne, I don't know how to say this, and it will probably sound really dumb or at least strange. But, well, I heard about you some time ago. I read every word in your file, and I have tried to find out everything I can about you. I just keep getting this feeling."

Cheyenne thought to herself, *Okay, Mrs. Lloyd, just get it out.*

I've been here before. But it seemed that Mrs. Lloyd was going to drag it out.

"Oh, there were a lot of people, like Judge Wentworth, who tried to discourage me from trying to adopt you. But you know, that feeling just won't go away. It felt right. I felt good about your coming into our home. My father always told me I had good instincts, and I should go with my feelings. So that's what I am doing."

Cheyenne couldn't take it any longer. "Look, Mrs. Lloyd, I understand. I'll be okay. I know how these things are. Temporary. I can be out of your house tomorrow."

"What?" asked Mrs. Lloyd, shocked. "I'm sorry, I have been rambling along and obviously not making any sense. I don't want you to go anywhere! What I want you to know is that in here," and she pointed to her heart, "I feel right about having you in my home. And now it's your home too."

"You mean you are not asking me to leave?" Cheyenne asked as she quickly wiped away a tear that was rolling down her cheek.

"No! Heavens no! Cheyenne, I've been trying to tell you, and not doing a very good job of it, that when I first heard about you, I got this feeling. I felt good all over. And now that I've gotten to know you . . . well, like my dad said, I've got good instincts. So I just wanted you to know why I filed the petition for adoption. I'm not some crazy old lady. It's just that deep down I believe the Lord led me to you. I just hope you are happy, that you understand that I think you are someone special, and I hope that someday you will want to be part of this family as much as I want you to be. I don't want to scare you. You've got all the time you need, and we will never finalize the adoption without your consent."

"You mean that you are asking me for my consent to the adoption?"

"Yes, Cheyenne. We would never push you into something you did not want to do."

Cheyenne looked at the beautiful woman sitting across the bed from her and wondered, *How can someone be so good? Why does she care about me?* Then she said to Mrs. Lloyd, "You are the best thing that has ever happened to me in my life, but I need some time, okay?"

As Mrs. Lloyd left the room, she reminded Cheyenne, "Hey, remember that tomorrow is Sunday."

Cheyenne knew what that meant. Two days after she had arrived in the Lloyds' home, it had been Sunday. She discovered that when Sunday morning rolled around, she had to be out of bed at 8 A.M. and be ready to go to church by 9 A.M. She did not get a vote in the matter. Mrs. Lloyd had informed her, "Around this house we go to church as a family and that includes you, Cheyenne."

Getting up on Sunday at 8 A.M. was not high on Cheyenne's list of fun things to do. But Cheyenne had another surprise once she got to church. Mrs. Lloyd informed her that the Sunday service was broken into three meetings, each about an hour long: one general meeting for everyone, then Sunday School for an hour with girls and boys her own age, and then still another meeting with just girls her own age. "Sounds great," she had said unconvincingly. Cheyenne just knew she would be bored to tears every minute of the entire three hours. *Isn't three hours forever?* she thought. She had not spent three hours in a church in her whole life.

She tried to make light of the three hours of church and jokingly said, "What are they trying to do, ruin the entire day?"

"Yeah, it is kind of fanatical, isn't it? Imagine spending three hours out of your week studying about your God," replied Mrs. Lloyd.

Cheyenne quickly replied, "No, I was just kidding. I didn't mean it like it sounded."

Mrs. Lloyd responded, "I didn't mean to be abrupt, Cheyenne. It's just that God matters to me more than just three hours a week."

Cheyenne spent three hours in church that day and every Sunday after that. She couldn't say going to church for three hours on Sunday was one of her favorite things, but it wasn't as boring as she thought it would be. And if she had to be truthful, she might even admit that she liked it a little. She also liked being included in the Lloyd family, but it made her feel vulnerable.

The more Cheyenne was around the Lloyds, the more she liked them. They were solid, blue-collar, hardworking people. The Lloyds were not wealthy people, at least not in worldly possessions. Richard was a college graduate and had just started his own business as a certified public accountant. Mrs. Lloyd had also graduated from college and taught school for a few years. Now it seemed that she was in charge of taking care of the neighborhood. There was never a day that she didn't render some kind of assistance to one of her neighbors. It varied from baby-sitting to shopping and everything in between. She even mowed lawns on occasion. Cheyenne didn't know how Mrs. Lloyd did it, but she always came away from the neighbors believing they had done Mrs. Lloyd a favor by letting her help. Mrs. Lloyd was a strange woman. *Too bad there aren't more people in the world like Mrs. Lloyd,* Cheyenne thought.

The Lloyds considered themselves to be middle-class Americans: average in every respect, and they liked it. Cheyenne came to believe the Lloyds were anything but average people. They lived in the Granite High School District in a new subdivision. The area was known around Salt Lake City for having some of the poorest families in the valley. That didn't bother the Lloyds, and it didn't bother Cheyenne. She knew she would fit right in with students from poor families.

One day Cheyenne came home to find the living room full of neatly folded laundry. "Let me guess," she asked Mrs. Lloyd, "you're starting a new laundry business?"

"That's a good idea, Cheyenne, but no, the laundry belongs to the Yates family who live two doors down."

"And you're doing it because . . . ?" Cheyenne asked.

"Well, their washing machine broke, and they are having

trouble finding a new one. So I said I would help her until she was able to find a new one," said Mrs. Lloyd.

"Why didn't she just go to the Laundromat?" asked Cheyenne.

"I couldn't let her do that. She has three kids and a new baby. Besides, how hard is it to do a few batches of laundry?" replied Mrs. Lloyd.

Cheyenne looked at her and shook her head. "A few batches?" Clothes were stacked everywhere.

"Cheyenne, I was just going to take the laundry over to her house. Would you mind helping?"

Cheyenne wondered how she could be so lucky.

Cheyenne was not an early riser by choice, and sometimes she didn't even bother to get up. In the past she had always missed her first class of the day—that is, if she even went to school that day. School started in less than a week. As Cheyenne walked into the kitchen, Mrs. Lloyd welcomed her. "I'm glad you're up. I was just going to eat. But now I'll have someone to talk to. I never got into reading the paper while I ate."

Cheyenne sat down and picked up her fork to start eating. Then she looked at Mrs. Lloyd, who folded her arms. "Cheyenne, would you mind saying a blessing on the food?"

Cheyenne was taken off guard. She had never said a prayer on food in her life.

"I'm sorry, Mrs. Lloyd— I mean, Nichole. I don't know quite how to. I've never said a prayer out loud before."

"Well, it's time we fixed that problem," Nichole said. "It's easy. It's like talking to your father—oops, I forgot. Well, it's like talking to me. First, you address your Heavenly Father, and then you thank him for any blessings he has given you, including the food you are about to eat. Then you ask him to bless the food, close the prayer in the name of Jesus Christ, and say 'amen.' There is no set format for prayer. You just talk to him."

Cheyenne said, "Um, well I'd rather not today. Why don't you just say it?"

"No, I don't think I'm going to let you off that easy. It's only me and you, so don't be shy."

Cheyenne said a simple prayer, but it came from the depths of her soul. When she finished, she looked at Nichole. "Thank you, Cheyenne. That was lovely."

Cheyenne wondered how Nichole was always able to make her feel so good about herself. The prayer was simple, not such a big deal, but to Nichole it had been more than a big deal. *How is it possible for someone to care so much for another?* Cheyenne wondered.

At one point in their conversation, Nichole said, "Cheyenne, umm . . . there is one more thing I have been meaning to tell you." She looked a little sheepish, and Cheyenne wondered what "little thing" Nichole had gotten her into now.

"And what would that be?" Cheyenne asked with a smirk forming on her lips.

"Well, I signed you up for early-morning seminary. That's a church class taught next door to the high school."

"But I thought my schedule was already full of classes that I need in order to graduate. How can I fit another class into my schedule?"

"Well, you see, this class is not taught during normal school hours."

Cheyenne groaned and asked, dreading the answer, "And what exactly do you mean when you say 'early morning'?"

Nichole had a smile on her face that turned into a slightly worried expression. "Well, since school starts at 7:50 A.M., early morning means seminary classes start at 6 A.M."

"Tell me you're kidding, that you don't mean 6 in the morning," Cheyenne pleaded.

Mrs. Lloyd just smiled and said, "Yes, I do mean in the morning. But I just know you are going to love the class."

"Me? Love a class that starts at 6 A.M.? You've got me mixed up with someone else again." Cheyenne rolled her eyes in disbelief and then added somewhat jokingly, "You know, living in the juvenile center might not be so bad after all."

Mrs. Lloyd laughed. "Oh, Cheyenne, it won't be so bad. Besides, one of my dear friends will be teaching your class."

Cheyenne drummed her fingers on the table. "Let's see. We go to church for three hours on Sunday, and now I *get* to go every day for another hour to a church class. That's a whole lot of church."

Nichole responded, "You don't have to go on Saturday. You can sleep in that day."

"You don't seem to do anything around here halfway, do you?" Cheyenne asked.

"I promise you, Cheyenne. You are going to love this seminary class. Your teacher's name is Jacob Wolfgramm, and I've already talked to him about you."

"Great! That means I'm in trouble before I even do something wrong," teased Cheyenne.

"No, I told him to make you the teacher's pet," said Nichole.

"I guess there's no hiding out around you, is there, Nichole?"

"What do you mean, 'hiding out?'" asked Nichole.

"Never mind. Are you going to make sure I'm up every morning?" asked Cheyenne.

"You can bet on that," said Nichole, who looked like a big weight had been lifted off her shoulders.

Then Cheyenne asked, "Do I dare ask what you have planned for us today?"

On Saturday night Nichole said to Cheyenne, "I have a favor to ask." Cheyenne was beginning to become wary every time Nichole started a sentence with those words. She asked with a smile, "Do I have a choice?"

"Um ... well yes, but probably not really," responded Nichole with a smirk.

"Okay, what have you got me into now?" asked Cheyenne.

"Well, you know how I teach the eight-year-olds in Primary. I would like you to come in and help me tomorrow."

"So now you are trying to get me to teach kids about God?" asked Cheyenne. "I don't even know what I believe about God."

"No, it won't be anything like that. Just come in with me and help. I'll do all the teaching. But I might ask you a few questions."

"I knew there was a catch in there somewhere," replied Cheyenne.

"So you will come and help?" asked Nichole.

"Did I ever have a choice?"

"I guess you didn't. But we will have fun. I promise you."

"You think I'm going to have fun teaching eight-year-olds about God?" replied Cheyenne.

"Trust me," said Nichole. "Those eight-year-olds will probably end up teaching both of us about God."

Nichole was the best. Cheyenne could never tell her no and she knew it. But she made her feel like she mattered. Nichole was magic. Cheyenne said, "I have one question. Why does everyone call you Sister Lloyd? I know that Mr. Roberts is not your brother."

Nichole laughed. "It's a term we use in our church when speaking to other members. You see, we all believe that we are brothers and sisters since we are all children of God."

Cheyenne realized she was beginning to like living in the Lloyds' home. She had never witnessed anyone show such love to so many people. And Cheyenne felt that she might even be included in her group. It was so different. Nichole somehow always found time to sit and talk with Cheyenne. In some ways, she felt that Nichole was becoming a friend. But then, what did she know of friends?

Cheyenne realized she had come to look forward to talking to Nichole. At times she caught herself telling Nichole about her past: personal things she had never told anyone. Then the next minute, she found herself withdrawn and wouldn't say anything but "yes" or "no." Cheyenne wondered how Nichole was able to sneak up on her so easily. Cheyenne caught herself several times and wondered why she was so easy to talk to. She wanted to trust Nichole. She wanted to be able to open up and tell her how she felt. But then the red flags would start flying. She thought talking to her was like being released from prison. It was definitely freeing, and yet when—if—it ended, she knew she would have a lot farther to fall.

Cheyenne tried telling herself to go with the flow, but then she would remember not to get herself trapped just because someone was nice. She had been there before.

Chapter 3

SEPTEMBER 4

The alarm blared. It was time to get up for Cheyenne's first day of school. It had been a long night, and she hadn't slept very well. She reached over her head and pulled back the curtains. It was still dark outside, really dark.

She looked back at the clock just to make sure it was really morning—*If you can call 5 A.M. morning,* she thought. She rolled out of bed and staggered to the bathroom. Once she got her eyes open and wasn't blinded by the bathroom light, she looked into the mirror, examining herself closely. Her face was passable, her jet-black hair was ugly, and she was too tall and skinny.

Cheyenne didn't stand in front of a mirror very often; she never liked what she saw. Besides, it was way too early in the day for a visual inspection, let alone any self-analysis. She turned the shower on ice cold. She knew that would wake her up. Then she reconsidered and went for the warm water, preferring comfort. She closed her eyes and let the warm water wash over her. In her mind she saw herself without make-up or dyed hair: a tall, thin, not-so-bad-looking blonde teenager who could pass as the Lloyds' daughter.

Dreaming again. I guess I should have gone for the cold water, she sighed.

"Tomorrow," she said out loud. "I'll think about that tomorrow. I don't have to decide anything today." Cheyenne knew she used that excuse way too often. Besides, introspection at this time of day definitely didn't make much sense.

She finished showering and dried off. Then she pulled on her black jeans, a matching jacket, and a V-neck T-shirt. She ran a brush through her hair a few times and decided she was ready for the first day of school of her senior year.

Nichole was waiting for Cheyenne as she came out of her room. Cheyenne was sure she still looked just slightly better than death warmed over. Squinting her eyes, trying to look less awake than she was, she said, "It's a little early in the morning for you to be up, isn't it? The sun doesn't even know it's morning yet."

"Good job, Cheyenne. I'm impressed. And you did it all by yourself. I told you it wouldn't be that hard."

"Then I don't look as bad as I feel," said Cheyenne as she looked through half-opened eyes. "Tell me how you manage to look so good this early."

"I'm not the hottie around here, Cheyenne. You should look in the mirror. Of course, you would have to open your eyes to do that," replied Nichole. She then continued on without taking a breath. "Cheyenne, I'm so nervous for you. Are you going to be okay today?"

"No big deal. I'm the resident expert at new schools. Remember, I wrote the book on it." In fact, Cheyenne had attended four different high schools as well as an alternative school over the past two years. She had learned to be adaptable—at school, as well as everywhere else, she had become quite good at blending in, not being noticed. Being there, but not so that someone would remember her. She shied away from making friends. She didn't want any ties. So going to a new school wouldn't be a big deal. But now things were different. She had always thought all she had to do was survive until she was eighteen, and then she would not have to report to anyone. Now she realized she could graduate. And then there were the Lloyds and their hopes and expectations. *I'll think about it tomorrow,* she thought to herself.

Mrs. Lloyd could see Cheyenne was troubled. She reached out and touched Cheyenne's arm. "Cheyenne, remember I'm in your corner. Okay? Anything. I'll be there for you no matter what. All you have to do is ask."

Cheyenne thought she was turning soft. She had to toughen up. "Thanks, Mrs. Lloyd. I'll be fine and I'll see you tonight."

"Wait!" said Nichole. "I knew you wouldn't have time to eat, so I made you this bacon and egg sandwich. Take it with you and eat it on the way. You'll be glad you did."

While walking to school, Cheyenne ate the sandwich. It was good. She thought back to the conversation she had had with Nichole the night before. "Cheyenne, I've gone over your grades and your test scores. You know, things just don't add up. It's like, two plus two will never make five. You are way too smart to be getting the average grades you have on your transcripts. So I asked myself, 'Why?' Now I'm probably not as smart as you, but it seems to me that you just never cared, that you chose to get average grades. Why?"

"I guess I never thought about it," Cheyenne responded. But she knew she was not being honest with Nichole. Getting average grades was just another way for her to remain hidden, out of the light, away from attention.

Then, just when Cheyenne thought Nichole was going to ask some more hard questions, she changed the subject as if she knew she had pushed hard enough. Then she asked, "Cheyenne, when you were a kid, did you ever dream you were Cinderella just waiting for the night of the ball?"

"You're kidding, right?" Cheyenne asked. "The closest I ever got to a ball was when I got hit in the face with one."

Cheyenne smiled when she remembered that Nichole had told her, "When I was a kid, I always had this dream that I would meet my Prince Charming just like Cinderella. But, alas, it didn't work out that way. I met Richard when he came into the Arctic Circle where I was working, and he wasn't even riding a white stallion. All he had was a blue Pinto. But that's not the point. Our dreams, whether they are in the day or night, whether they are just hopes or even goals, help push us along, help motivate and inspire us. I believe that if you can't dream it, you can't do it."

Nichole thought for a long moment and then added, "Cheyenne, don't be afraid to have dreams."

"Sometimes I wonder about you, Nichole," Cheyenne said.

"Well, you're not alone because I wonder about myself all the time," replied Nichole.

Cheyenne looked at Nichole and wondered if this person was real. Her feelings were doing flip-flops, and she was having trouble dealing with them. Seventeen years of experience told her to withdraw, to protect herself, protect her feelings, jump behind the wall. Yet the past weeks had almost undone her. She was perplexed, confused, and sure she didn't know anything except that the lovely blonde lady sitting next to her on her bed loved her. Nichole had been trying very hard to be her friend . . . or was it her mother? Cheyenne knew she would have been a different person if Nichole had been her mother. Nichole didn't seem to be anything but good. She accepted Cheyenne with all of her flaws. *Darn, just when I thought I had it all figured out,* Cheyenne thought.

It was then that Cheyenne noticed that Nichole's eyes were misting a little. "Is something wrong, Nichole?" Cheyenne asked.

Nichole brushed her hand across her cheeks, laughed, and sniffed. "No, nothing is wrong. Everything is right. I want the best for you, Cheyenne. You deserve it."

After a minute of silence, Nichole said, "Cheyenne, tomorrow is going to be a big day for you. I hope it goes well. Is there anything I can do to help you get ready for tomorrow? Do you need anything?" Nichole then slipped Cheyenne a twenty-dollar bill and said, "Put this in your purse. Call it your panic stash. Use it when you have an emergency or chocolate attack."

"I can't take your money. And really, Nichole, I'm okay, but I'm a little worried about you."

Then they both laughed. Nichole said, "Cheyenne, there is something else I have been meaning to give you. It's been my good luck charm for years. But now I want you to have it." With that, Nichole reached behind her neck and unfastened her necklace. She motioned for Cheyenne to stand and turn around while she put it around her neck.

Cheyenne looked in the mirror and saw a beautiful gold pendant. It was heart shaped, but the heart had been broken in half and then welded back together again. You could see the broken line. It was strange but lovely.

"But, Nichole, I can't take this. It's yours."

"And now it is yours, Cheyenne. It has meant a lot to me for many years. I hope it is as lucky for you as it has been for me. It has a story, and someday I'll tell you all about it."

She reached out and took Cheyenne's hand. "You will never know what having you here has meant to me. See you in the morning." She turned and quickly left the room.

Again Cheyenne felt warm all over and had a giant lump in her throat. She was so happy and yet confused. She felt like laughing and crying at the same time. She couldn't remember the last time she had cried. Nothing had ever mattered that much.

Long after Nichole had left Cheyenne's room, she had lain awake on her bed, unable to get Nichole and all those confused feelings off her mind. Things weren't the same as they had been only a month earlier. Nichole seemed to be able to look past all the problems Cheyenne had had in her life to see only the good things. Nichole believed that Cheyenne was a beautiful young woman. Cheyenne wondered if she could ever live up to Nichole's expectations. Then something that had been said in church the week before struck her. "It doesn't matter how many times you fall off the horse, only how many times you get back on. Start living today. Forget the past. Start anew." It made sense, but still, Cheyenne was afraid.

Cheyenne asked herself again, *Am I really afraid? Why? Of what?* She was almost to school but couldn't shake the nagging questions.

She remembered a discussion she had had with Susan, one of her social workers. "Cheyenne, before you can make any changes in your life . . ." What was it she had said? It was something like, "First must come the change of heart." Cheyenne reached up and touched the pendant, which was warm against her chest. Susan had explained, "You can only change when you decide inside that you want to change. You can't change because someone else wants you to change."

But before Cheyenne could change herself, she knew she needed hope. She remembered that the same speaker in church had said something about hope. It was like, "First, one must have hope."

Cheyenne knew that every time she had really wanted something in her life, it had gone away. Did she now fear the loss of hope that the Lloyds promised? Was that her problem?

Cheyenne tried to shake the thoughts out of her head as she continued into the seminary building. She was ten minutes early for class. She really had been amazing herself lately. She couldn't imagine her old self early for a class that started at 6 A.M. It was not possible. She sat on the couch in the foyer, her mind swirling.

What was it that Nichole had said about seminary? Nichole had said, "Look at it this way, at least it's only fifty minutes and not three hours long like church."

Cheyenne had responded, "Yeah, but it's five days a week. I'll be so churchy or so bored within a week, I'll go crazy."

Nichole laughed, and then she said, "Your seminary teacher is a Polynesian guy, Jacob Wolfgramm. You are gonna love him. He grew up right down the street from me. I've never met anyone like him. He's brash, straight forward, a great storyteller, really good looking, and mean. You cross him, you could get thrown through the wall. So try to get on his good side, okay?"

Then she added, "Just kidding! He is the nicest guy you will ever meet. The way Jake tells his own story is that he was born 'in a hut on a dirt floor in Tonga.' I think he is making that up, but at least it sounds good. He claims to have come to this county when he was eight and couldn't read, write, or speak a word of English. Turns out that he almost became a gang leader. But then his seminary teacher got hold of him, and three years later he was elected student body president of Granite High. He's a survivor. He grew up in a house where they didn't have a shower. The water heater never worked, so he always got to school early so he could shower in the gym. He never had any money, but he didn't let any of that stop him. If he decided he wanted something, he just went out and got it. He found a way.

"He reminds me of you in so many ways, Cheyenne. He is now at the University of Utah, a star football player, and he was just elected student body president. I spent many hours talking to Jacob when he was in high school. I was a friend he could talk to. Everyone needs one of those."

Nichole laughed just remembering. "You see, he was good at wrestling. His coach became concerned when he suddenly started missing practice. Finally, the coach confronted him. Jake answered, 'Coach, I want to come to practice, but my dad thinks I'm old enough to work and quit playing kids' games. He told me I would have to practice on my own time, not when there was work to do.' His dad owned a small construction company and used Jake whenever he could.

"The coach talked to his dad and worked it out so that Jake could go to practice whenever there was not work that had to be done. And by the way, Jake won the state wrestling championship that year. He always seemed to find a way.

"Cheyenne, you need to be careful. Whatever it is he has, it might be contagious."

"Yeah, I can see it now. Introducing our homecoming queen, Cheyenne Carson."

But inside, Cheyenne squirmed. Good things didn't happen to her. She wasn't like Mr. Wolfgramm. She had never been a winner.

Cheyenne thought, *Is change possible?* She had to shake her head again as if the shaking would cause the crazy thoughts to tumble out. *I'll worry about that tomorrow*, she thought again.

Cheyenne knew it was time to make her not-so-grand entrance into the seminary class. The class was half full, and the good seats in the back were almost gone. She also noticed that the teacher was greeting each of the students as they came through the door. He asked them their names and tried to make each feel like a welcomed guest. He was polite, in a masculine sort of way, and he laughed a lot. Cheyenne waited for two kids to pass in front of her and trailed quickly behind them, hoping to slip past Mr. Wolfgramm and find a chair out of harm's way. She was good at doing that. She turned her chin down, her eyes to the floor, and tried to slip by Mr. Wolfgramm as he spoke to the kids in front of her. But he saw her and stepped directly in front of her, blocking her path. He didn't move and didn't say a word. Finally, Cheyenne raised her chin and looked directly into his eyes. He said, "I'm so glad you made it to my class. What did you say your name was? No, let me guess. You're Cheyenne, right? Cheyenne Carson."

Cheyenne smiled slightly and nodded but wondered how in the world he had known her name. She hurried away and found a seat in the back corner of the room as far away from everyone as she could get and tried to vanish. She didn't look around but kept to herself. She didn't say a word to anyone. It was easier that way, drifting in and out without anyone even knowing she had been there. She had slipped back into her old habits. *Some change*, she thought.

She learned it was Brother Wolfgramm, not Mr. Wolfgramm, when he introduced himself. Brother Wolfgramm started class soon after that. He told a few jokes and asked the class members to introduce themselves. Suddenly there was a loud commotion in the hall. The door flew open and banged against the wall. In walked the best-looking guy Cheyenne had ever seen. He looked like he had walked right off the beaches of Santa Monica and was dressed as if he had stepped out of the pages of *GQ*. With wildly curly blond hair that seemed to have a mind of its own, he was definitely surfer material. It was obvious he knew everyone was looking at him, and he liked it.

Looking at Brother Wolfgramm, he said, "I'm sorry for the interruption, but since it's the first day of class, I figured you would cut me a little slack. Besides, I'm new around here. My name's Harrison Daniels, and yours?" He asked, reaching out to shake Brother Wolfgramm's hand.

Brother Wolfgramm shook his hand and said, "Everybody gets one mistake, Mr. Daniels. You can take that chair right over there."

"How about this chair instead?" he asked. "The surroundings seem to be nicer." He sat in a seat between two girls, taking time to look each girl over as he sat down. The attention of the class deteriorated, and groups began talking to each other. Some students were laughing. It was apparent that Mr. Surfer GQ couldn't care less if he had caused a disruption.

Brother Wolfgramm continued, but it wasn't a minute later that he stopped. Mr. Surfer GQ was talking to Andrea, the girl sitting to his right. Brother Wolfgramm didn't say a word but just stared at Harrison. It took about a minute for Harrison to realize that Brother Wolfgramm had quit speaking and was looking at him. Kind of laughing he said, "Sorry, was I speaking too loud? Just being friendly."

Brother Wolfgramm knew he had to get control of the class again. The whole year depended on maintaining some kind of order and respect from the outset. He bit his tongue and said, "Mr. Daniels, that's twice. If you want to talk, I'll sit down and you can take over. If you want me to do the speaking, then I expect a little courtesy from you."

"No problem. Just trying to make a new friend."

Brother Wolfgramm went on speaking, but then Harrison started to talk to Heidi, the girl on his left.

Then something happened that surprised the class, Cheyenne included. Brother Wolfgramm didn't say a word. He bent over, opened the bottom drawer of his desk, and pulled out two pairs of boxing gloves. He threw one pair to Mr. Surfer GQ and said, "You look like a big strong boy who can handle himself. Here's the deal. If you can stay off your back for one minute, I'll give you twenty bucks and you can go buy a Coke and a donut. If you don't, you will sit in that chair right over there and not say one more word. Now, you have a choice," he continued, "it can happen right here in front of everyone, or we can go out back where you won't be embarrassed. Do you understand me, Mr. Daniels?"

Harrison looked at the chiseled frame of a football player who was playing seminary teacher. He tossed the gloves back to Brother Wolfgramm, trying to bait him. "I didn't do anything but try to be friendly. How come you're so uptight? Besides, I'm not here to fight. I'm here to learn about the Lord. Aren't you going to teach me?"

It was apparent that Brother Wolfgramm didn't intend to babysit anyone, and he wanted everyone in his class to know he meant business. He put the gloves away, glaring at Harrison. "Next time you won't have a choice, Mr. Daniels. You are welcome to stay as long as you don't cause another disturbance."

Cheyenne knew Mr. Surfer GQ's type: good looking and arrogant, cocky and probably rich, all in one dose. He was too much to stomach even if everyone voted him Mr. Popularity, Best Looking, or whatever. Cheyenne didn't want anything to do with him. Of course, someone like him wouldn't want anything to do with someone like her either.

The class had grown silent. It was apparent that Brother Wolfgramm wasn't going to be pushed around. With that, he continued with the introductions. Then he went right into his lesson. There wasn't any laughter or a word muttered by any of the students. They paid attention to the whole lesson. It wasn't hard though. Brother Wolfgramm was a great storyteller, and Cheyenne was surprised when the bell rang and the class ended. Maybe seminary wouldn't be as bad as she had thought.

Cheyenne watched as Mr. Surfer GQ, almost bigger than life, spoke to both girls after the class had ended. He took the opportunity to run his fingers through his unruly hair while he continued to speak with them. Taking Heidi's arm, he guided her out of the room. Cheyenne noticed that Mr. Surfer GQ didn't look Brother Wolfgramm's way as he made a quick exit, something she bet he didn't do very often. It was a game he was playing. He wanted to push just as hard as he could. He was just testing Brother Wolfgramm and Cheyenne knew it. But she also realized that Brother Wolfgramm wasn't going to play his little game.

Cheyenne stayed clear of any conversation with the students in the rest of her classes. She also avoided eye contact with them, as well as with her teachers. She responded only when asked a question, but she kept thinking about what Nichole had said: "School is not a have to, it is a get to." Nichole expected her to succeed in her classes. *Why not give it a shot,* Cheyenne thought.

Cheyenne watched the other students closely. She noticed there was an in-crowd—a group of kids who dressed nice, tried to do well in school, and mostly kept together. Then there was the crowd that just hung out, that didn't want to be in school. Cheyenne related to that group but wanted to avoid it. Then there were a whole bunch of kids who didn't really fit into either of the two groups. That was where Cheyenne wanted to be—invisible. Then, of course, there was Mr. Surfer GQ. He was a group unto himself.

It had been a long day by the time Cheyenne finished her last class. She had started her day long before the sun had come up, and now, walking past the gym on her way home, she wasn't paying much attention but mostly just thinking. Suddenly, a big, stupid lurch dressed in football pads came running around the corner of the building and knocked her flat on her back.

She looked up and recognized him immediately. It was Mr. Surfer GQ himself. He looked down at her and said, "I'm sorry. Are you okay?" After looking her over and realizing he was not interested, he added, "You should be more careful and watch where you're going. You could get hurt around here."

It was obvious she would never get a permit to even visit his world. He didn't help her up or assist with her books. "Sorry," he said, "but I've got to run or I'll be late for practice."

With that he jogged toward the football field. He had not recognized Cheyenne from seminary. She knew he never would, and she liked it that way. She didn't want to be recognized or remembered. Nonetheless, she added that to the list of reasons that she didn't like Mr. Surfer GQ.

Cheyenne's books and papers were scattered across the grass. She got into a sitting position when she noticed someone had started to gather her books. It was Brother Wolfgramm, her seminary teacher. He reached over, offered his hand, and easily pulled her to her feet, almost lifting her off the ground.

"Cheyenne," he said, "you're just the person I was trying to find. I hurried back down here after my classes at the U, before football started, hoping I could talk to you. Would you come over to the seminary building with me for a minute?"

Cheyenne looked at him as if considering the request. "Well, only if you promise no more religion today." And she gave him a sly smile.

Once inside the seminary room, he sat down at the desk and motioned for Cheyenne to sit in the chair in front of him. As she sat down, he smiled at her and said, "I guess you are curious as to why I would want to talk to you."

"As a matter of fact, I am," she responded without emotion.

"Well, you see, I have a problem. I really don't know many of the students, not personally or by name, and I need some help. I need an assistant to help me with the administration of the class."

He didn't even pause for Cheyenne to say anything. "Anyway, this morning in class, I looked around wondering whom I should ask to be my assistant. The minute I saw you, I knew you were the person I needed to help me. I have a very busy schedule at the U and, from time to time, I will need some help. What do you say?"

"You want me to help you? What are you talking about?" Cheyenne was dumbfounded and almost speechless. Then she found her voice and stammered, "You don't know a thing about me. I don't even think I really want to be here. I could never be an assistant to anyone, let alone a seminary teacher. Besides I don't even know if I believe in God."

"Thanks, I knew you would do it," Brother Wolfgramm replied.

"But I said I don't want to do it."

"I know what you said. Do you know what I said when they asked me to teach this class? I said no in about the same way you just told me no, and here I am teaching in spite of it."

"So what does that have to do with me?" Cheyenne asked. "Besides, I might be better at saying no than you."

"Well, it's like this. Maybe I was inspired, or maybe I just knew you could help me. Besides, then you could be the teacher's pet. Either way, you already are. Oh, by the way, Nichole kind of volunteered you. She told me you would love to help me."

"You're crazy! I can't help you," Cheyenne said, still looking anywhere but at Brother Wolfgramm.

"Look at me, Cheyenne," he said. He waited until she turned and looked at him, and then he continued. "Everyone who comes through the door to my class matters. I may not know what your life was like before you walked into my classroom, but you know what? It really doesn't matter. In my eyes you are no better or worse than anyone else in the class, that is except for maybe Mr. Daniels. By the way, that was Mr. Daniels who knocked you down, wasn't it?

"Yeah, I think so," Cheyenne said.

"Did he even say he was sorry?"

"Not really. He told me I should watch where I was going."

"He needs a blanket party," mumbled Brother Wolfgramm.

Cheyenne looked puzzled. "A blanket party?"

"Yeah, you know, a few guys throw a blanket over his head and beat the tar out of him."

Continuing on, he said, "I've heard good things about you, Cheyenne. I know Nichole really well. She is one of my most favorite people in the whole world. She called and talked to me about you. She thinks you are a keeper. Me? I think you are one lucky young lady to be living at the Lloyds.'"

"I'm beginning to believe that, Mr. Wolfgramm," Cheyenne said. "And just what did she tell you about me?"

"She told me that you are drop-dead gorgeous, smart, very talented, that you try to please everyone, and that you are outgoing and the life of the party. She also said you would say no if I asked you to be my assistant but that you would really mean yes. By the way, call me Jake, not Mr. Wolfgramm."

"I know, I know. Mr. Wolfgramm sounds like an old man, right?" Cheyenne replied. "I've already had that lecture."

"So you see, you really don't have a choice. You can't say no."

"But I can't do it! I don't know what to do, and I don't know one person in the whole school."

"That's the easy part. I'll teach you as we go along what you have to do. But we may have to make it up on the run. I don't know either. This is the first time I've done this too," Jake admitted. "Oh, and did I tell you that you might have to teach a few classes for me when I have to be gone?"

"What? There's no way. I quit! Get yourself a different assistant!"

Jake laughed, "Just kidding."

"You . . ."

Cheyenne was flustered. But before she could say no again, Jake said, "Thank you. I'm glad to have you as my new assistant, Sister Carson. Now, here is a list of the students in the class. As your first assignment, I want you to prepare a roll so you can keep attendance for me."

"But how can I keep a roll? And when did I become your sister?" she asked.

"Tomorrow, first thing, I will ask everyone to stand and tell us their name. You can fill out a seating chart. It will be easy, like falling off a log. Cheyenne, we're going to make a great team, I just know it. I'll see you bright and early in the morning, and don't worry about it, I'll cover the lesson tomorrow."

With that he got up and tossed Cheyenne a can of soda, which she dropped. And then he was gone. Alone, she sat there wondering what had happened to her and her quiet, little, insulated world, the one no one ever visited. Now it seemed that everyone was just barging in without even knocking.

School seemed to fly by that week. Cheyenne was busy. It was easy to keep up in all of her classes; and as strange as it sounded to her, she actually thought all of her teachers were okay. But she still had to deal with Jake every day. He was always giving her a hard time. He seemed to get a kick out of knowing what made her squirm, and he found something new for her to do every day. Nevertheless, Cheyenne found herself enjoying her time in seminary. Jake was so full of life. It was easy to see why Nichole liked him so much. He was infectious. *Yeah,* Cheyenne thought, *like the plague.*

Cheyenne laughed as she went out the door. "See you next week, Mr. Wolfgramm, umm, Jake, I mean, and don't be late for class. I had to make excuses for you every day this week."

"Hey now, I was on time, at least for a Tongan."

Cheyenne had a little lighter step as she walked home that day.

Chapter 4

SEPTEMBER 26

"It's good to see you," said Brother Forester as he stood and shook hands with Jake. Come in and sit down. I've been meaning to drop by and chat with you. I've had so many good reports. I must have had five or six parents call and go on and on about you. I can't thank you enough for taking the class. And I understand your attendance has gone up each week."

Jake threw a sealed envelope on Brother Forester's desk. Brother Forester looked quizzically at the envelope. "What's this?"

"That's my letter of resignation."

"What? I thought things were going great in your class."

"They are now. I wrote that letter after the first week, and I almost brought it up and gave it to you then. At first I was frustrated. It was like I was talking to a bunch of third-graders. They wouldn't respond to questions. All I saw were blank stares. I couldn't get a discussion going; I didn't think the kids heard a word I said. I wasn't sure they would tell me their own names if I asked them, and I really thought I was wasting my time."

"Jake, it takes high school kids some time to get to know and trust you. I'm glad you chose to give it a little time. Remember, you didn't open up to me the first day I dragged you into my office."

"You're right, but I didn't remember that, and you have to remember that I'm kind of slow."

"We all know you aren't slow, Jake. Stubborn, maybe, but not slow."

"Anyway, little by little the kids started to participate, and now I can't shut them up. And their questions sometimes blow me away. They are so perceptive and innocent. There are some kids that still don't know why they get up in the morning, but there are others who are stretching themselves, really trying to discover and learn. It throws me back to when I was your student. I keep remembering my own experiences and feelings. I can tell that some of my kids are going through the same struggles I went through. You know, it's like I can relate to how they are feeling.

"An amazing thing has happened, Brother Forester. I find myself really caring about some of my kids. I want to help them understand and really be there for them. It's so exciting to see them grow, step by step. Some of these kids just have a way of crawling under my skin. You know what I mean?"

"Yeah, I remember watching you scam kids out of quarters in order to be able to buy lunch. It took me a long time to figure out what made you tick. Then I had to convince you that you were on the wrong track. You weren't what I'd call an easy sale."

Jake responded, "Right now I have two kids, the Carson girl and the Daniels kid, that I can't get off my mind. I want to grab them and shake them. I want to tell them who they are and what they could be. I want to wake them up. They are both loaded with potential. Maybe it's because they remind me of me. I wasn't that bad, was I?"

"What do you think, Jake?"

"Brother Forester, why did you do it?"

"Do what, Jake?"

"Why did you pick on me when I started high school? Why me?"

"I felt it in here," Brother Forester said as he pointed to his heart. "After that I just didn't have any other choice."

"So what do I do now?"

"Follow your heart, Jake. It wasn't me asking you to teach this class, it was the man upstairs. He obviously wanted you and not someone else. You must have the key."

"And what key would that be?"

"The key to their hearts, Jake. But then you already knew that, didn't you?"

"Well, I may have a key, but it's not turning any of the locks I've tried."

"You'll figure it out. It's amazing how much you can care about certain kids in such a short time, isn't it?"

"Sometimes it's all I can think about, Brother Forester."

"That's because you care, Jake. Keep it up. I knew you were the right man for the job."

"That's it? That's all the advice you have for me?"

"You don't need any advice, you just wanted someone to talk to. I'm here for you anytime."

"I've got just one more question."

"What's that?"

"Are you sure you're not a locksmith?"

Jake had remained a faithful alum of the Granite High football program. He loved his old coaches and tried to help them whenever he could. Right now Granite was in the middle of an extended losing streak. The previous year the school set a record for consecutive losses, not just in the history of the school but also for any school in the state of Utah. Worse, it didn't look like the streak would end anytime soon.

One day Jake found Coach Grundy after practice. "Hey, Coach, you got a minute?"

"Sure, Jake. What do you need?"

"Tell me about Harrison Daniels."

"Where do you want me to start?"

"Tell me what you think about him."

"Harrison has the skills to make this team a winner, and I believe he can play at the next level. He's that good. But he has the 'I' problem. Everything is centered on him. I have tried to talk to him, but it's like talking to that wall over there. He moved here from California last summer, and he has the attitude of a blond-headed surfing champion. He knows everything, including that he is one of the best high school quarterbacks in the country. He was not very happy when his father made him enroll here. He never wanted to leave sunny Southern California, but his father had a change of employment and brought Harrison with him. His father, not Harrison, chose Granite because he knew Harrison would play quarterback here. His father doesn't care if we ever win a game. He knows the scouts will flock to see Harrison every time he steps onto the field. Believe me, he is that good."

Jake started pacing and said, "Well, he certainly looks the part. I'd say he's about six-foot-four, and I'm guessing he weighs around 210 pounds, without an ounce of fat on his body. I heard he ran a 4.4 forty. That by itself puts him in a whole other world as a quarterback. I also heard that some Pac-10 schools and even some from the Southeastern Conference are looking at him. I know Utah has put him on their wish list. So, coach, what do you think about his arm?"

"Jake, that kid throws footballs like he's launching rockets."

"Does he have any academic problems?" asked Jake.

"Well, his transcript from California shows nothing but A's with all of the academic classes you can take."

"Sounds like one in a million, Coach," said Jake.

"No question about it. But he won't amount to a hill of beans as a person until he figures out that some of us also inhabit this planet."

Jake stopped Harrison after seminary. "Harrison, could you

come by here tonight about 7 and talk to me?"

"What do you need, Brother Wolfgramm. You can talk to me right now just as easy."

"Harrison, I don't have time right now, but I'll see you here at 7 tonight."

That night, Harrison drove up in a brand-new Beamer for his appointment with Jake.

"Glad you could come by, Harrison. I try to meet with all of my students one-on-one. I want to get to know you guys on a more personal level. I've heard so much about you from Coach Grundy that I had to see if it was all true. Then I went to one of your practices, and I was impressed. Do you plan to play college football?"

"Yeah, I always thought I would play college ball somewhere. That is until I landed here. It's going to be impossible for anyone to see me perform here. This team is so bad. No wonder they have the longest losing streak in the state. It's impossible for a pass play to develop because no one knows how to block. And if I were able to get a pass off, we don't have anyone on the team who could catch it. I think my dad was all wrong. He thought it wouldn't matter where I went to school. I think he is going to turn out to be dead wrong. No one is going to see me here."

"I see you're driving a Beamer, Harrison. Nice wheels."

"Yeah, I told my dad that if we were moving to Utah, he had to at least buy me a new car."

"You are lucky. I don't think there is anyone else at Granite whose parents could afford to buy a car like that."

"You're probably right. My dad has made a lot of money because he's smart. You know, in this country, we can be anything we want to be if we have any brains and are not afraid of a little work. I don't have much sympathy for poor people. I think most of the kids on the football team are perfect examples of people who just don't care or want to work."

"Don't you think you might be a little harsh in your judgment, Harrison?" asked Jake.

"Listen, Brother Wolfgramm, I came down here to talk to

you because you asked me. If you need me to do something, then just ask and I'll do it, but don't preach to me."

Jake breathed deeply and said, "I'll be at your game tomorrow since I don't have practice at the U the day before my games. I want to watch you play. It's your first game, isn't it? And by the way, let me know if you want to come up and watch the U play. I might be able to get you some tickets."

With that, Jake got up, held out his hand, and said, "I'm glad I got to talk to you, Mr. Daniels. I'll see you in the morning."

Jake watched Granite lose its first game of the year to Olympus 27–7. It wasn't pretty. Olympus played its second and third teams most of the second half. Early in the first quarter, Harrison dropped back to pass, saw a hole up the middle, and scored on an impressive sixty-seven-yard run. He was quick and powerful.

From that point on, Olympus marked Harrison with two defensive players and ignored most of Granite's other offensive players. The defenders' sole assignment was to bird-dog Harrison—go where he went and make sure it wasn't very far. As a matter of fact, he ended up on the ground almost every play, but he kept getting up. Granite's line had more holes than a sieve. Harrison didn't have time to do anything but chuck and duck once he got the snap. But every time he got knocked down, he got back up. It appeared that some of Harrison's teammates started to give him some respect.

Harrison hit receiver after receiver with bullet-like passes right on the money. The only problem was that nobody could catch them. He threw one pass that traveled sixty yards in the air. Jake noticed several college scouts watching the game. They seemed impressed. Maybe Harrison's father was right after all. Harrison didn't need to win to be seen, he just had to play.

Toward the end of the second quarter, Reggie, one of the wide receivers, took the heat of Harrison's fury when he trotted back into the huddle after dropping another spiraling pass. Harrison screamed at Reggie. "You've got to catch those!"

At halftime before the coaches came into the locker room, Harrison continued his harangue. He was shouting. "You've got to play this game with your heart. When somebody knocks you down, you've got to get back up and knock them down on the next play. If you drop a pass the first time, you've got to catch the next one. To win you've got to want it and want it bad. What I see out there is a bunch of guys who don't care."

Through gritted teeth, Sione, a large Polynesian, muttered, "Hey, rich boy, one more word out of you today and you'll wish you'd never heard of Granite High School."

Harrison replied, "I wished that a long time ago." He then stormed out of the room, kicking a garbage can over as he left.

Sione watched him walk away and said loudly enough for him to hear, "Rich boy, you're all talk."

Just before the start of the second half, Coach Grundy caught up with Harrison. "Some of the things you said in there needed to be said, but you are the wrong one to say them, Mr. Daniels. So you're sitting the second half. Then I want to meet you in my office at 7 in the morning. Don't be late."

The next morning Harrison walked into Coach Grundy's office at 7 sharp, slouched down in the chair, and waited. Grundy was already there. He got up and closed the door before sitting behind his desk. "Harrison, you know you might just be the best player who ever played at this school. But I don't care if you are the best player in the whole state. You talk to your teammates one more time like you did yesterday and you won't ever step onto this field again. There isn't any 'I' in team. Do you understand me, son?"

Harrison looked at Coach Grundy and with a mocking smile said, "The problem isn't me, it's this team. I thought the things I said at halftime might motivate some of the guys. I'm sorry if

I was out of line. I was so frustrated. I didn't even have time to throw a pass. They had ten guys in our backfield before I even got the ball."

"You're right, Harrison, but you were wrong in the way you handled it. I think most of the guys hate you for being so good, but on the other hand I think they were beginning to gain a little respect for you after you kept getting up after every play without complaining. You could turn in to a real leader, but you have to give them time to learn to trust you, to follow you. Do you understand me?"

"I understand. So what do you want me to do?" he replied.

"While the team practices tomorrow, you will be running around the track. I want the rest of the team to see you running. We have to get some discipline on this team, and you are going to be my example. But while you are running, I am going to talk to the team about the things you said. I hope that when I am through, the team will believe that you are their leader. Then all you have to do is act the part."

Grundy left the words just hanging in the air. Then he added, "Maybe with your help we can break the streak. Are you willing to try?"

"I'll try, but I don't see much hope."

"Don't forget to bring your running shoes tomorrow," said Grundy.

Harrison wasn't in a good mood. He barged out the door and turned quickly down the hall. He slammed his fist against a locker and said, "Why did I have to come to this worthless school? The only people who go here are morons, dropouts, or just plain losers!"

Just as he finished his tirade, he turned the corner to walk down the hall. But he stepped on something, stumbled, and fell. He didn't see the girl sitting on the floor with her legs stretched out, and he barely saw the floor before he made a perfect five-point landing, nose first. Blood immediately started flowing from his nose. He rolled over, grabbed his nose to stop the bleeding, and looked back to see a girl sitting there looking shocked.

Cheyenne put her book down and started to laugh.

"What's so funny?" Harrison growled.

"I don't know, but if I rated your landing, it would be a 5, maybe top out at a 6. Maybe you should be more careful and watch where you're going?"

"Me? Don't you have someplace better to sit? Besides, a little sympathy would be appreciated since it's your fault I fell!"

Cheyenne threw a tissue to him. "This may help. I don't want you to ruin your fancy clothes." She got up, started walking away, stopped about ten yards down the hall, turned, looked at him, and said, "You are something special, Mr. Daniels. Glad to finally meet you. I've heard so much about you. With a little luck I won't have to do it twice." With that she turned, walked away, and didn't look back.

Harrison muttered to himself, "Man, who was that witch? She looked like . . ." He stopped in midsentence. "I know her from somewhere."

"Hey," he yelled at her as she was about to turn the corner of the hall. "You didn't tell me your name."

Without turning around Cheyenne said, "No kidding, Tonto!"

Chapter 5

OCTOBER 27

Cheyenne had not missed one class in eight weeks, and that included seminary. And to her amazement, she was at least fifteen minutes early for seminary every day. She blamed that on Jake. She had volunteered, army style, to help Jake get the classroom ready for each day. He told her that helping set up the class was part of her job as his assistant, and she didn't mind. She had begun to look forward to her time with Jake. In the beginning, he carried on a one-sided conversation. She tried to avoid getting caught up with his infectious personality, but that didn't last long. Once he got wound up, there wasn't a lot of dead time. Before she realized what was happening, she was talking as much as Jake. She told him things about her life she had never told anyone. He sneaked up on her. She wasn't sure how he had done it, but when she realized what was happening, she decided she had found a friend—Jake was someone she trusted, someone she could talk to, and someone with whom she could identify.

Cheyenne liked Jake. There was just no way around it. He always pestered her, teased her, challenged her, and made her think. He laughed a lot but mostly at himself and his own dumb jokes. Nichole had been right about him.

As Cheyenne walked into class one day, Jake motioned to her and said, "Sit down for a minute, Cheyenne. I've already got the class ready. I want to tell you a story."

"Do we have time? I mean, class starts in twenty minutes." Cheyenne looked at her watch, trying to sound convincing, "That doesn't give you much time. Why don't we wait until tomorrow?" she teased him, knowing he was going to tell her anyway.

He went on as though she hadn't said a word. "As you know, I came to this country when I was eight years old. The first day I arrived in Salt Lake, my parents made me go to school. I was in the third grade. Now remember, I had never been to school and I didn't speak or write one word of English. So I struggled. I couldn't go home and get any help because my parents didn't know English either. I've had to struggle my whole life with the language. To this day, test taking is very difficult, and I don't always do well."

"And the point of your story would be?" Cheyenne asked. She continued on without waiting for his answer. "Let me guess. You had a lot of difficult challenges in your life, and you found a way to succeed despite those problems, right?"

Jake waved off her attempt to be funny. "Cheyenne, sometimes we get the feeling we are all alone, that no one has to face the hurdles we face each day, that no one understands how hard it is for us. Sometimes it's nice to know there are others who also have to struggle through life."

"And you don't think I've done very well dealing with my problems?" Cheyenne asked.

"Tell me, Cheyenne, how do you think I felt when I had to come to high school and shower before school every day because we didn't have a shower at home? How many excuses do you think I made up when someone found me showering in the locker room before school in the morning?"

Cheyenne replied, "Well, I would probably think my family was on the bottom of the financially successful list, while you, on the other hand, would probably believe that you were on the top of the lucky list because you were able to use the shower at school."

"Like I said, Cheyenne, you are a lot smarter than me. You're right, though. It's not the problems that make or break us, it's how we deal with the problems that are thrown at us."

Cheyenne suddenly became introspective. "Jake, tell me what made you come out fighting instead of quitting? What made you want to make something of yourself instead of joining some gang or working on a construction crew?"

"I've thought a lot about that question, Cheyenne. What do you think made the difference?"

"I believe you are either born a fighter, or you are not. I think it is something innate we have within us. You must have a fighting spirit, and, well, I don't know about me."

Jake was silent for a long time. He finally said, "For me it was a mentor, someone I looked up to, someone who cared about me, someone who wouldn't give up on me, someone who tried to show me the way."

"Is that what you're trying to do for me, Jake?"

"You don't beat around the bush, do you, Cheyenne?"

"Jake, there is one main difference between the two of us, and that's called family. You always had someone standing in your corner. I didn't even have a corner."

"So you think not having a family is the cause of all your problems?" Jake asked. "Let me tell you another story."

"You said one story, and this will be your second one. You are only allowed one story a day, remember?" Cheyenne teased.

Jake didn't even slow down.

"I was about twelve, working with my father doing some roof repairs on a residence. My father said, 'Get me a shovel,' in language that was barely audible. So I got down off the roof and brought him back a shovel. When I got back, my father took the shovel and whacked me across the arm, knocking me off the roof. While I was lying on the ground, he said to me, 'Next time don't walk.' I was lucky to hit a bush on the way down, or I could have really been hurt. I knew, though, as soon as I hit the ground that

I had better get back up on the roof as fast as I could."

"But he still loved you, Jake. He just had a different way of showing it."

Jake knew he was in a battle of wits, and he wasn't going to give in. "And that was another problem. In our culture, we are taught to react with physical force first and maybe talk later. So how do you think I reacted when some kid in third grade made fun of my speech problems?"

"Let's see. You punched him several times, I imagine, and he never did it again, right?"

"And how do you think my teachers reacted?" asked Jake.

"They probably called the principal, and the principal called your parents. Right?"

"And what do you think my father did when the principal made him come to school because I was in trouble for fighting?"

"Probably patted you on the back and asked you how bad you thrashed the other guy," Cheyenne replied.

"Close, but before that he beat the tar out of me."

"So you were in trouble one way or the other?" she asked.

"You're beginning to get the picture, Cheyenne."

"But somehow you overcame those problems to become a big shot at the university."

"You don't get it, Cheyenne. I still have all kinds of doubts about myself. I am very insecure. I am still self-conscious about my speech problems. You see, Polynesians have trouble forming words that have a vowel followed by a constant. As president of the University of Utah student body, I still struggle almost daily when I have to speak in front of a group. I used to feel sorry for myself. I thought if things would have been different, I would have been a good student. I thought I never had a chance, that no one liked me, that I was stupid. But then I decided I was just afraid— afraid of being embarrassed."

Cheyenne thought for a minute and asked, "So you think I just feel sorry for myself because I never had a family?"

Jake smiled at her and said, "I'm just telling you about me. I didn't say anything about you. But someone once told me that to succeed in life you have to leave a little blood on the mountain."

"You mean I have to suck it up? No pain, no gain. That kind of stuff?"

"Cheyenne, I just think you have learned to protect yourself. You probably have good reasons. I know if you let your guard down, you may get a little bloody. But you know, it might just be worth the risk."

"That's easy for you to say," Cheyenne replied.

As they were both sitting there, they heard the bell ring. Jake finally interrupted Cheyenne's self-imposed quandary. The twinkle in his eye and the smirk gave him away. He was the biggest tease Cheyenne knew.

"Hey, Cheyenne, I heard that Robert—what's his name? You know, that guy in your English class? He's just dying to ask you out. Has he talked to you yet?"

"I don't have a Robert in my English class," Cheyenne replied.

"You're not sure, are you, Cheyenne? Are you are calling my bluff?" Jake asked. "Take my word for it, he's going to ask you to the junior prom."

"Jake, do you stay awake nights thinking up things to tease me about?"

"Hey, if he doesn't ask, two other guys told me they are dying to ask you out."

Cheyenne shook her head, laughed, and said, "Jake, you are impossible."

Ignoring her comment, he continued, "And you've also been holding out on me."

"What do you mean?" Cheyenne asked.

"My sources tell me that you have the highest grade in your English class. Right?"

"Umm, I don't know," Cheyenne said.

"Cheyenne, you're getting an A in English. And you have A's in every other class, don't you?" Jake said.

"Maybe. What makes you ask? Are you writing a book?"

"I have this theory, Cheyenne. Want to hear it?" asked Jake.

"No, but I have the feeling you're going to tell me anyway."

"There was this beautiful little girl who always seemed to draw the short stick in life. She felt picked on and probably had a right to feel that way since she was an orphan. She bounced around from school to school, house to house, always just getting by—a C in math, maybe a B in English, nothing to write home about. The problem is that this girl was smart, very smart, but she didn't want anyone to know it. She never looked people in the eyes. She tried to blend in with the group so no one would even notice her. She didn't want anyone to even remember she had been there. Average grades, average person. No one noticed."

Cheyenne rolled her eyes and started straightening some papers, trying to ignore Jake and his story. It was just a little too close to home.

"Now stay with me, Cheyenne."

"Jake, you are nuts. I think you must have had a bad dream."

"Now this girl even tried to dress and appear like someone ordinary but a little off beat, someone you wouldn't notice, or you wouldn't want to notice. That way, it was easy for her to hide out in plain sight. What do you think, Cheyenne?"

"Did you say you were majoring in storytelling at the U?"

"Cheyenne, don't back off now. You're showing me a little spunk, maybe even a little fight. I'm proud of you. I'll bet you haven't told Nichole about your grades, have you?"

"It's a little early yet. The final grades aren't out."

"Let's see. Very smart, perhaps witty, infectious, and bordering on good looking. It's getting harder and harder for you to hide out, Sister Carson."

Cheyenne didn't know why it was so easy for Jake to embarrass her, but at the same time, he made her feel good. She knew he liked her. She also knew he was in cahoots with Nichole. They did the old tag team—one during the day and one at night. Both tried to build her up and make her feel good about herself. They wanted her to know they cared. It seemed funny to her, but lately she would catch herself looking in the mirror when she passed, wondering. She knew she was not good looking; her legs were too long, and she was too tall and too skinny. No, she didn't feel pretty. But she still caught herself looking and wondering.

On her way home from school, Cheyenne stopped at the drug store. She thought to herself, *It's now or never.*

The stop at the store made Cheyenne a little late getting home. Nichole met her at the door. She looked a little nervous.

"I was beginning to worry about you," she said. "I was about to start looking for you."

"Did you wonder if I had taken off? Run away?" Cheyenne teased.

"Cheyenne, do you know how much you mean to me?"

Cheyenne saw that Nichole had noticed the shopping bag in her hand that she was trying to keep out of sight.

"Everything's okay. I . . . I just had to stop at the store," Cheyenne replied as she tried to make a quick exit. She was not eager to talk, not now. Cheyenne was as nervous as Nichole but for a different reason.

"I'll talk to you in a minute. I need to change." Cheyenne hurried into her room before Nichole could ask her any more questions.

Cheyenne thought, *If I'm going to do it, I may as well get on with it before I chicken out.* She quickly changed into some sweats and hurried into the bathroom. Cheyenne had just turned the water on to cover up any noise she made when she heard a knock at the door.

"Cheyenne, let me help you. You can't do that by yourself."

Cheyenne opened the door and asked sheepishly, "How did you know?"

"It's just one of those girl things. Now, let's call my friend Amber. She'll know what to do."

Several hours later, Amber was drying Cheyenne's freshly cut and new honey-colored hair.

"I can't tell you how long I have waited for this day," Nichole finally said. "Okay, you can see it now, if you're really nice. Close your eyes and hold onto the chair so you don't fall off."

Nichole held the mirror in front of Cheyenne, who stared into it for a long time. Her hair was now soft blonde, its natural color. Cheyenne almost didn't recognize her own reflection. She was shocked. "I don't know. It doesn't look like me."

"Cheyenne, you look like a doll. Now let's get out my makeup. I've got some great colors that will work with the new, softer you. You are going to knock 'em dead tomorrow. I'm telling you, tomorrow there are going to be a lot of heads turning and more than one guy asking, 'Who's the new chick?'"

They laughed. Cheyenne hesitantly asked, "Do you really think I look okay?"

"Cheyenne, you look great."

There won't be any hiding in the shadows tomorrow, Cheyenne thought.

Later that night when Mr. Lloyd came home, Cheyenne was lounging in the recliner reading a book while Nichole was working in the kitchen. He walked into the kitchen, hugged his wife, and whispered loud enough for Cheyenne to hear, "Who's the babe?" pointing to the recliner. "One of Cheyenne's friends?"

Cheyenne tried to keep a straight face but ended up laughing. "Does everyone in this house think they are a comedian?"

Richard, directing his attention to Nichole, said, "I guess I'll have to go to school with her tomorrow and sit through every one of her blasted classes. Otherwise, she might not make it home without five boys trailing behind." Then he said to Cheyenne, "Don't you be giving out our phone number, or we'll be buried in calls."

During dinner, both Richard and Nichole continued to talk about Cheyenne. She was embarrassed but loved every minute of it. It felt so good to have two people care about her, wanting her to feel good. Cheyenne wondered, *How? Why me? What did I do to deserve this?* She had never been shown so much affection.

Cheyenne went into her room that night feeling great; she

was nervous about the next day, but she still felt good. She opened her closet and dug out the clothes she had vowed never to wear, the ones Nichole had purchased for her after they had left the courthouse. Nichole had been right. The day had come when she would use them.

Cheyenne tried on each outfit while standing in front of her mirror. She even struck a few poses. As she was trying the clothes on, a thought struck her: *Oh, no! I'm going to have to face Jake in the morning. He will be ruthless!* "Heaven help me!" she said out loud. Then again, maybe the attention would be okay. "Jake, you are such a pain—but a nice pain," Cheyenne said to herself.

She selected a sky-blue turtleneck sweater and some white jeans that showed off her long legs. They were still too long, but she laid the clothes out, all ready for the coming morning.

The next morning, Nichole was up and waiting when Cheyenne came into the kitchen to get something to eat. Her hair hung almost to her shoulders and ended in a little outward flip. Nichole smiled and said, "I'm so excited. I can hardly wait until tonight. I want to hear everything that happens—every detail. Promise me."

Nichole appraised Cheyenne. Slightly taunting her, she asked, "By the way, I seem to recognize those clothes. Did you check them for moth holes? Actually, if I do say so myself, they are quite cute. And, Cheyenne, you are beautiful."

Cheyenne didn't know how to respond, so she grinned and asked, "What did I do to deserve you, Nichole?"

Nichole immediately responded, "I could ask you the same thing!"

Cheyenne felt panicky. She was so excited, so nervous, and so full of anticipation when she left the house that she almost felt like she was walking through a fog. She braced herself as she walked into seminary, trying to act as if it were just a normal day. She wasn't sure what Jake would say, but she knew he would not let her slip quietly into class. Not today.

Jake glanced up as Cheyenne walked through the door, and then he turned back to the lesson he had been reviewing. Suddenly, he jerked his head up and began to stare. A huge grin spread across his face. Without warning, he slowly leaned back in his chair and kept going backward until he fell flat on the floor, feigning shock and disbelief. Cheyenne ignored him and went about getting the chairs in order. He got up, dusted off his pants, staring at her all the while. Finally, he said, "Cheyenne, is that you? I don't believe it. I'm speechless."

"Well, I guess there's a first time for everything. I've never seen you speechless," Cheyenne responded. "What's the matter? Have you got a sore throat?"

"No! I just thought I recognized you. But no, it couldn't be. Hair the color of harvest wheat, a sky-blue sweater, long, slim legs. For a minute, I thought you were . . . but no, it couldn't be."

Cheyenne continued her cleaning routine, trying not to play into his hands. "Jake, get a grip."

"Cheyenne, your hiding days are over. Back row or corner, there isn't going to be any place for you to hide any longer. I promise that you will be noticed today by more than one person, and may I be the first to tell you that you look spectacular?"

"Jake, you make such outrageous statements. I mean, how can I tell when you're telling the truth?" she asked. She tried to keep from smiling. She was enjoying his attention.

That wasn't so bad, Cheyenne thought, even though she knew her face was three shades of red. *I might just make it the rest of the day. In fact it might be fun.*

Then Jake said, "Now, tell me the truth. Did someone attack you last night while you were sleeping?"

Cheyenne sneered; she wasn't taking the bait. "No, and I don't look so different, *Mr.* Wolfgramm," she replied.

"Different? Are you kidding? Just watch the boys when they walk into the room if you think I'm kidding. Someone is going to ask me who the new girl is. Bank on it."

"Oh, stop it, will you?" Cheyenne responded. "You know I get embarrassed easily. Don't make a spectacle of me in front of the class, please. Promise me."

"Okay. You know me. Mum's the word. Believe me, I won't say a word. But you look great."

Cheyenne sat down front and center, right in front of Jake's desk. "You're not funny," Cheyenne said, trying not to smile.

He looked at her with a smirk, and raising his hands, he asked, "Moi?" Soon, other students began to arrive. Cheyenne tried not to notice, but everyone who came in took a second look and then stared at her as they took their seats. Cheyenne was nervous, flustered, and embarrassed. She felt like getting up and running away, but at the same time it felt kind of good to have people notice that she was alive.

Right after the opening prayer, Jake said, "Class, we have a new student, whom I need to introduce, and I would like each of you to say hello and introduce yourself to her today as you leave class. And you guys know the rules, no dates on the first day. Miss, umm, what did you say your name was?"

Cheyenne was totally embarrassed. She muttered, "You're not very funny. Besides, you promised."

The class laughed and someone said, "Cheyenne, is that really you?" There were a few catcalls before Jake regained control of the class.

"Now see what you did?" Jake commented. "You guys embarrassed her!"

Cheyenne wanted to do something, and so, without thinking, she stood and faced the class. "Since our teacher thinks he is a comedian, let me take the roll, and then, *Brother Wolfgramm*, you can give us the lesson."

Cheyenne finished taking the roll, counting thirty-five students, twenty more students than had originally enrolled in the class. She knew why the class was growing. It was Jake. He made seminary come alive. He made the Lord seem real, and Cheyenne almost always felt that he was talking just to her. Of course, he made everyone feel that way. Cheyenne caught herself wondering when she had started feeling and caring.

After class ended, several students walked by and said, "Hi, Cheyenne, are you available Friday night?" and laughed. Mr. Surfer GQ was the last person to leave the class. He walked across the room straight to Cheyenne's desk and asked, "Don't I know you from somewhere besides this class? It seems like I've met you before." He was trying awfully hard to be nice, but Cheyenne wasn't buying it, not today.

In a terse voice, Cheyenne responded, "No, I don't believe I've ever had the opportunity to meet you before. I'm one of those losers, those misfits, who couldn't go to any other school, so I ended up here. Come to think of it, I do remember seeing you before, or someone who looked like you. But no, that guy had blood all over his face. He wasn't watching where he was going. He was very unathletic and boring."

Jake interrupted the standoff. "I didn't know you two knew each other. That's good because I want you two to team up. I don't have a lot of time right now, but let me just tell you that I've chosen you two to head up our Sub-for-Santa project this year."

Harrison looked befuddled, and in no uncertain terms, he stated, "Me? No way! I'm too busy! I don't have time to help some welfare family!"

"Good," Cheyenne responded, "because I wouldn't work with this over-inflated bag of wind, this egomaniac, if you paid me."

Jake had on his no-nonsense face. "I don't believe I asked either of you if you *wanted* to be in charge of our project. What I said was that you two are *going to* head up our Sub-for-Santa project. I am going to discuss my plans with the class next Tuesday. That night, I want to meet with the two of you at seven, in this classroom. Do you understand? We will have a planning session. Both of you think about it until then." With that, Jake walked out of the classroom, leaving Cheyenne stunned, fuming, and silent. GQ stood there with his mouth open. No one had ever told *him* what to do!

Cheyenne looked up at Harrison and said, "Close your

mouth. It's not polite. But don't worry about it because I will never work on any project with you."

Harrison grinned at Cheyenne. "My, you're a little feisty. Can I have your phone number? I forgot mine."

"You need some new lines. That one's been around for a long time. Maybe you should check with your writer," Cheyenne responded.

"How about letting me treat you to a burger and we can discuss the Sub-for-Santa?" he asked, undaunted.

Cheyenne couldn't believe her ears. This guy never gave up. Talk about an ego. But he was sadly mistaken if he thought she would spend any time with him. "Not even in your dreams," she said as she stood, picked up her books, and marched out of the room.

Harrison laughed and called, "See you Tuesday night. I'll give you a lift home after the meeting." He watched, his mouth still open, as she left the room.

Two days later, Harrison was leaving the gym when he noticed Jake sitting on the bleachers. Jake had the day off from football and had stopped by Granite on his way home.

"Got a minute?" Jake asked. Harrison walked over and stood facing him. "Sit down," Jake directed. It was not a request but more of a directive. "Harrison, have you ever heard of permanent potential?"

"What do you mean?"

"Well, it's someone who has potential but never rises above the ground-floor level. Forever full of potential, and that's it. Permanent potential. Right now, that pretty well describes your approach to life."

Harrison, not to be outdone, leered and sarcastically responded, "Now that you've told me how much you like me, what is it that you want to talk to me about?"

"Harrison, you're the man! The only problem is that you haven't figured out which man you should be. I think you could be a real leader in this school instead of its number one jerk. I'm not giving up on you, not yet. That's why I want you to work on our Sub-for-Santa project. I want you to use your head and come up with a plan that doesn't center on money. Maybe you'll even learn something from this project. Maybe Cheyenne can teach you a thing or two about life."

"I'd *like* her to teach me some things," Harrison responded.

"You may be the man, Harrison, but you've got some real surprises in store for you," Jake said. "You have no idea, but you'll find out. Believe me, you'll find out."

"Well, as long as it's Cheyenne teaching me, it could be interesting," replied Harrison.

"She'll teach you, all right, and it's something you need to learn. But it's not what you're thinking. Let me give you a little advice. Hang on, Harrison. This could be the ride of your life."

Chapter 6

NOVEMBER 6

The walk home from school was invigorating. The cool November air hinted of winter and was refreshing. Cheyenne was proud of what she had accomplished in the first quarter of her senior year, but what mattered more was that she had someone to tell, someone who cared perhaps even more than she did. It was true what they said: "Even a great art masterpiece isn't of any value unless you have someone to share it with."

She felt like Maria singing in *West Side Story,* "I feel pretty, oh so pretty . . ." except that she didn't feel pretty—she felt pure delight. Her report card read straight A's. Her English teacher had written a note that said, "Outstanding student. You should consider writing as a profession." Cheyenne couldn't wait to show Nichole.

Cheyenne wondered whether she was excited because of her report card or because she got to show the report card to Nichole. The implications caused her to think about Nichole. Was she a friend? A mother? *Just how important has this lady become to me? How important have I become to her?* Cheyenne had always put off addressing such questions until tomorrow. *Was tomorrow here?*

It seemed that her tight little circle of one had slowly expanded. No sooner had she thought of how proud Nichole and Richard would be than she thought of Jake. She could see it coming—embarrassment, plain and simple. And what would Judge Wentworth say? Not that she would include him in her circle, but she thought of what he had said about kids like her never making it. Maybe he had been wrong. Maybe she would show him.

Cheyenne's days were always full now. As she hurried across the street to get to her house, she remembered Mr. Surfer GQ's antics. Just thinking about him made her furious. "The audacity of that conceited jerk," she said under her breath. But then, she wasn't about to let him ruin what had been one of the best days of her life.

Cheyenne almost ran into the house but stopped short and took a second to catch her breath. Then she strolled leisurely into the kitchen. She found Nichole doing some ironing. "Hi," Cheyenne said matter-of-factly as she sat down at the table and started eating the snack Nichole had prepared for her. She was intentionally ignoring Nichole's expectant stare. Cheyenne knew Nichole couldn't stand the wait much longer. It was Cheyenne's turn to tease. She opened her book as if to start reading. Nichole began tapping her fingers impatiently on the ironing board. Finally, Cheyenne asked nonchalantly, "And how was your day, Nichole?"

Nichole was almost frothing with anticipation. "Okay, Cheyenne, you've got three seconds to spill the beans. You know I've been waiting all day to hear what happened."

Cheyenne started to giggle, and then her giggle turned into laughter. She laughed until her side hurt and tears ran down her cheeks. Nichole knew she had been set up. She punched Cheyenne in the arm. Cheyenne fell out of the chair, still laughing. Finally, Nichole, attempting to be stern, said, "Now start with seminary and tell me everything, and don't leave out anything. Do you understand?"

"Okay, okay, okay. Let's see. Well, how's this for starters?" she said, getting up and holding out her report card. Nichole snatched it out of Cheyenne's hand and looked it over. Then a tear rolled down her cheeks. Cheyenne stood up, not knowing what to say, feeling like she had just won the lottery. Nichole reached out her arms and drew Cheyenne into an embrace. "I am so happy for you," she said. It took a minute for Nichole to regain her composure. She wiped her cheeks and said, "First thing I'm going to do is mail—no, I'm going to take a copy of this to Judge Wentworth. I can hardly wait to see the look on his face. What does he know about teenagers? The second thing I'm going to do is to put your report card right here on the refrigerator door for everyone to see. I might even blow it up in size. The third thing we are going to do is make Richard take us out to dinner tonight to celebrate! And we are going to stuff ourselves with real chocolate dessert at a really nice restaurant, *before* the main course."

Cheyenne waited patiently for Nichole to calm down. "Okay," Cheyenne continued, now that you've got that out of your system, are you still interested in the rest of my day?"

"Do I need to sit down?" Nichole asked.

"Probably," Cheyenne said, grinning. "It was like . . . like . . . nothing I could imagine. For starters I had two boys ask me out today."

"You didn't!"

"Yes! But only one counts. One was that Surfer GQ guy, and he didn't really mean it. And Robert—I don't know his last name—was the other guy. He seems nice, but I have never noticed him before today. I don't know anything about him."

"Isn't the GQ guy Harrison Daniels, the football player everyone is making such a fuss about?" asked Nichole.

"Yes. But I'm not going to ruin my day by talking about him."

Cheyenne hurried on so that Nichole couldn't ask her any more questions about Harrison.

"Anyway, after English ended, Robert came up to me. He was nervous. He introduced himself and, without even taking a breath, started talking about the novel our class is reading. He never even looked at me. I knew how he felt since I am not very good at this dating thing either. Then, almost in midsentence, he bumbled and blurted something like, 'Cheyenne? Would you go . . . um, to the dance me with this Friday? I mean would you go with me?'

"He was really blushing. He is kind of cute; he's one of those guys you would expect to see reading a book at a football game. But he was nice! Then he said, 'Cheyenne, you look really nice today. I almost didn't recognize you. I've been meaning to talk to you all year, and today . . . well, today . . . you . . . you just look extra nice today.'

"I laughed and told him I'd love to go to the dance with him on Friday. I really was excited just to be asked to a dance. Then I added, 'Robert, what did you say your last name was?'"

Nichole continued asking questions, making Cheyenne recount the whole day, detail by exciting detail. While Cheyenne was talking, Nichole turned off the iron and sat with her elbows on the table, cradling her chin, listening intently to every word. For Cheyenne, it was like reliving the entire, wonderful day all over again. And it was because of Nichole, because she got to tell Nichole, and because Nichole wanted to hear every single detail. It was a new and exciting experience for Cheyenne.

When Cheyenne ran out of words, Nichole continued to look at her. Cheyenne waved her hand in front of Nichole's eyes to get her attention.

"What a great day," Nichole finally said, smiling.

Cheyenne looked content, and it felt like her heart was ready to burst. Then Nichole got a sly look on her face. "So I take it you're interested in this GQ guy? Come on, come clean. Tell me everything."

"What?" Cheyenne exclaimed. "What makes you think I'm interested in that jerk?"

"Cheyenne, you can't slide that one by me. Remember, it

wasn't that long ago I was where you are now. Let's hear it all."

"Nichole, you've got this one figured all wrong. I'm not interested in Harrison. It's Jake! He's forcing me to work with the jerk. Talk about an egotistic, chauvinistic, male . . . pain! Harrison is the opposite of everything I would look for in a guy."

Nichole smiled. "You like him that much, huh?" She started laughing.

"Come on, Nichole. It's not like that at all. I admit he is the big football star and is probably going to college on a football scholarship. He comes from a lot of money, drives a fancy, new sports car, and the girls are always fawning all over him. I admit he's good looking. However, in his case, beauty truly is skin deep. This guy is looking out for number one. He doesn't care about anyone or anything except himself. Besides, he drools."

"He's cute, huh?"

"Why do you think I call him Mr. Surfer GQ? He looks like he just stepped out of a fashion magazine," Cheyenne responded.

Nichole looked at Cheyenne and said, "Okay, so has he asked you out?"

"Well, he asked me to go get something to eat. He also wants to bring me home after our meeting with Jake next week. But it'll be a cold day in . . . well . . . it'll be a cold day when I agree to get into a car with Harrison Daniels."

"Cheyenne, remember, this is me you're talking to. You wouldn't care so much if you didn't like him just a little," Nichole said with a wry smile.

It took a minute, but finally Cheyenne asked a question that had been nagging her for some time. "Nichole? Let's say someone, some boy, and *not* Mr. GQ, is really nice. And let's say I even like him. What happens when he finds out about my past? Could he or anyone else really be interested in me? I'm a nobody with a criminal record."

"Cheyenne, you're the best! My only concern is if there is anyone good enough for you."

"There you go again. You're looking through blinders again.

Don't you get it? I'm not the person that you keep talking about."

"Oh, but you are, Cheyenne. Oh, but you are. If you only knew." Nichole grinned mischievously and asked, "So what are you going to do when the hunk tries to bring you home after your meeting on Tuesday?"

"I told you, I would never get in a car with him, even if it is a BMW."

"Yeah, but you say it with such passion. I mean, if you really don't care about him, you wouldn't care if he were a jerk or an egomaniac. It would just be a ride home, wouldn't it? Maybe you should give him a chance. Let him bring you home. What can it hurt? That is, if you really don't like him."

"Aaaagh, boys! They're nothing but trouble," Cheyenne complained. "And here you are encouraging me."

"You're right. They can cause a lot of trouble, but sometimes it's nice to have them around. You know, to take out the trash, cut the grass—that kind of stuff," Nichole joked. "Cheyenne, listen to me for a minute. I want you to quit being so hard on yourself. I want you to quit living in the past. In ten years, I want you to look back on this year of high school and remember it as one of the best years of your life. You are a beautiful young woman to behold, but inside, you're even better. And always remember that you are a child of God and that he loves you, even more than I do."

Tuesday night came quickly. Cheyenne was so nervous that she couldn't sit still; she was pacing, sitting, standing, and every once in a while, groaning. It was almost time to leave for the meeting with Jake and Harrison.

Nichole watched Cheyenne stew. She was grinning when Cheyenne looked at her. Nichole changed the smile to an indifferent look, and then she laughed. Cheyenne made a face at her.

As she fussed, she thought of the things she needed to take

with her when she left home. *Did I say home?* she wondered.

Nichole laughed again. "Cheyenne, you have gone in the bathroom three times to check your makeup and your clothes. You just brushed your hair again and stopped in front of the hall mirror. You even made faces at yourself. Now tell me how much you dislike this jerk you will be seeing at the meeting. By the way, you look nice—way too nice to be going to some boring planning meeting."

Cheyenne grimaced, and then she smiled. She knew she was lucky to have someone like Nichole, even if she was having way too much fun at Cheyenne's expense.

Cheyenne flippantly responded, "Did Mr. GQ pay you off too? Remember, I told you I'll be walking home. I'll never get into his car. And you can take that to the bank."

"Which bank?" asked Nichole.

When Cheyenne arrived at the seminary building, Jake was already in the classroom, sitting across from Harrison. She felt her breath catch a little. "I do not like him. In fact, I can't stand him," Cheyenne said to herself. "I am not interested. I'm not interested. I said, I'm *not* interested."

"Hey, glad you could make it," said Jake. He stood and pointed to the chair next to Mr. GQ. "Have a seat."

Before sitting, Cheyenne moved her chair next to Jake's so she was also facing Harrison. She knew she wouldn't feel comfortable sitting that close to him. Jake watched her move the chair. When she was seated, looking somewhat uncomfortable, he said, "I knew I had the chair in the wrong place. Thanks for fixing it for me, Cheyenne."

Jake's statement hung in the air for a full minute.

"Well, as I told you earlier," he finally continued, "what I want to do for Christmas this year is a Sub-for-Santa. I would like our class to take on the responsibility of providing Christmas for one family. Now, my concern is that I know that most of the students in our class simply don't have any money. That's where you two come in. I want you to figure out how we can balance those two factors. How can we provide Christmas for a whole family and not spend a lot of money?"

Harrison looked as perplexed as Cheyenne felt. Jake continued, "However, the most important goal I want to achieve is for each student to feel the true spirit of Christmas, the spirit of giving."

Cheyenne thought about what he had said. "Let me see if I understand what it is you are proposing," she said. "You want us to provide a full Christmas for a whole family without spending any money, and while we do this you want us to understand the spirit of giving?"

"That's right, Cheyenne. You see, we have to find a way to reach beyond ourselves, to give something that stretches our souls, while at the same time making sure we provide a wonderful Christmas for this family."

"I think that is what you call a conundrum," Cheyenne said. "Do you have any suggestions?"

"That's why you two are making the big bucks," Jake joked. "But when this project is over, I want each and every student to be proud of what they were able to give or do this year, even if all they can give is something used, or whatever. I want everyone to put some real thought into the gift they give to this family, but I don't want them to spend a lot of their own money. It's up to you two to come up with the ideas and plans for how we can really make this thing fly."

They all sat there waiting for someone to say something. Finally, Cheyenne asked, "Why me, Jake? I don't have any experience in this kind of thing. Besides, I do the chairs every morning for you."

"This is not about experience or money. For someone like you, Harrison, going out and buying a present would not be a problem, but that is not what anyone is going to do. The gifts have to be something from your heart. Cheyenne, you face a different problem than Harrison, but in some ways it is the same.

The reason I chose you two to be in charge of the project is that you come from opposite ends of the food chain. I hope you can blend your backgrounds in a way that can make this project meaningful for each student in our class."

He waited a minute and then added, "I expect both of you to spend some time thinking about what I said, and probably some time on your knees. Have either of you got any ideas off the top of your heads?"

They were both silent. Cheyenne thought about what Jake had asked. Finally, she said, "Jake, you are right. I've never done anything like this before. But you know, this year there have been a lot of people who have given to me, and I think it is about time I figured out how to give back. I'm going to try to figure this out, and I'll do the best I can, but I'm not sure how good it will be. You know, lack of experience."

It was obvious that Harrison wasn't getting the message when he added his two cents' worth. "Hey, it's easy, Brother Wolfgramm. Some of the kids in the class have parents with money. Now, I know you don't want us to think about money, but if we do have money, we can buy some really nice presents. Others can go out and beat on the doors of local retailers and ask them for a donation for the cause. It's no big deal."

Jake shook his head. "You don't get it. That is exactly what I don't want to happen. I want each and every gift to matter. I want it to mean something not only to the person who receives it but also to the giver. It's not about how big, how nice, or how expensive it is, it's the intent of the heart that is put into the giving of the gift."

Cheyenne was almost overwhelmed by the task Jake had given them. She knew that he was serious, but she didn't have a clue where to begin. She sighed, looking at Harrison. "Jake, I'm not sure you've got the right people for this job. Please reconsider."

"Cheyenne, you underestimate yourself and quite possibly Harrison. I want you both to take some time and think about it. I want you to tell me your ideas at our next meeting. Tomorrow I will talk to the class and tell them about the family. We can call them 'Our Family.'"

Jake studied his two pupils and said seriously, "I expect you both to put some effort into this project. It matters. Tonight I'm going to go visit the family I've picked out and assess their situation. I'll brief you and the class tomorrow morning. Don't say anything about the project. I would like the class to think that they thought of the idea."

"Whatever," said Harrison.

Jake responded, "And, Harrison, I don't like young ladies out walking the streets at night. Would you please give Cheyenne a ride home?"

"I'd love to give her a ride home," Harrison replied. "I was actually planning on it."

Cheyenne stood up, looked at both of them, and said, "I'm not riding home with him. Not on your life!"

"Come on, Cheyenne. I'll be on my best behavior," Harrison pleaded.

Jake tried to take control of the situation. "What do you have against Harrison?" he asked.

"How long do you have?" Cheyenne retorted.

Jake studied her for a minute and said, "Look, Sister Carson, you're my responsibility, and I want to make sure you get home safely. If you won't ride with Harrison, then I will have to take you home. It's not only out of the way for me, but I don't have time."

Cheyenne was steaming. At least she thought she was mad, though she didn't really feel mad. "All right. You two win. But it's straight home," Cheyenne insisted.

"Scout's honor," Harrison replied.

He politely reached over to take her arm as they walked to the car, but she pulled away. "I don't need your help. I'm not an invalid," Cheyenne said. He shrugged. When they got to his car, he opened the door for her and closed it before walking around to the driver's side.

Cheyenne had never been in a car that looked like this one.

She was amazed by its simplicity and beauty. At the same time, she was desperately trying to control her heartbeat. She couldn't decide if it was because she was mad or if she was catching the flu. Her stomach was twisted in knots, and her temples were pounding.

Harrison was on his best behavior. He asked for directions to her home. Cheyenne didn't dare say anything except where she lived. She was trying to get control of her stomach, head, and breathing. She couldn't remember being this upset. But then, she couldn't remember ever having this kind of a reaction because she was upset at someone. After a minute, he turned to look at her. "You sure you don't want to get something to eat?"

Cheyenne cut him off without hesitation. "You promised. Straight home."

"All right, all right," he said. "You're a bit touchy when I'm around. What did I ever do to make you hate me?"

"You really don't have a clue, do you?"

"No. Did I do something to you?"

"Well, aside from tripping over me and then blaming me for your bloody nose, and running over me while you were in full football gear, and scattering my books across the grass without apologizing, and thinking that the world revolves around you. Need I go on?"

"What? What are you talking about?" he asked.

"Think about it, but don't get a brain cramp. Stop here. That's my house," Cheyenne said, trying to control her voice. He stopped the car and started to get out. Cheyenne didn't wait for him to come around and open the door. She bolted up the walk without looking back. He leaned against the car, watching her leave. Cheyenne knew she shouldn't be rude just because he was, so she turned when she got to the door and said, "Thanks for the ride."

As she stepped onto the porch, she saw Nichole sitting by the window watching for her to come home. When Nichole saw her, she scrambled across the room, trying to make herself seem inconspicuous. Cheyenne stormed through the door, trying to look put out. Her heart was still racing and her stomach was upset. To top it off, she knew Nichole had seen her get out of his car. *I'm in trouble now,* she thought.

Nichole looked up and watched Cheyenne try to calm herself. "I'm glad I didn't go to the bank," she said, "because I could have sworn that was a boy who brought you home tonight. It wasn't Mr. GQ, was it?"

Cheyenne was at a loss for words. She was unhinged and excited. She walked around in circles, clenching and unclenching her fists. Before she could say anything, Nichole said, "That's the guy you don't like, right?"

Cheyenne headed for her bedroom, not knowing what to say. She felt like a child throwing a tantrum, but she wasn't sure why. "That guy, oh, that guy . . . " she said, and her words were cut off by the door slamming shut.

Nichole sighed and said to Richard, "I think someone has discovered boys."

Cheyenne felt fit to be tied at seminary the next morning. She hadn't slept well. She just couldn't figure out why she was an emotional basket case, and that bugged her. Could she have feelings for the jerk other than disliking him? She went over every detail of the previous night, trying to figure out why he bugged her so much.

Cheyenne avoided looking at Harrison when he came into the room. After he was seated, she tried to sneak a glance, but he saw her look at him and he winked. She quickly looked away, feeling like she had been caught trying to steal a cookie out of the cookie jar. *Darn, he winked at me. Who does he think he is?* she thought.

Jake stood to begin the class. There were at least forty kids today; the room seemed to be bursting at the seams. When Jake stood, all the students gave him their attention.

"Guys, I've been thinking. I want our class to do something

really special for the holidays. I have this feeling . . ."

Without raising his hand, Craig Divet stood up and asked, "Jake, do you think we can do one of those Sub-for-Santa things? You know, like for some needy family?"

There was a chorus of "yeahs!" Jake wanted it to be their project. He wanted them to come up with the idea, and they had. He surveyed the room and then asked, "Do any of you know of any needy families?" He looked at Cheyenne and winked.

Cheyenne thought, *What's with everyone winking at me today?* She knew she was totally out of control. She knew right then that she was having one of her "Blonde Days"—and they were legitimate now. She couldn't be held responsible for anything she said or did today.

The students began talking among themselves, and the consensus was that they didn't know how to go about choosing a needy family.

Finally, Jake interrupted them. "It just so happens that I know of a family," he said. "I visited with them just last night. Now let me tell you about them. They are the nicest people, but they have fallen on hard times through no fault of their own. They have six beautiful children—three boys and three girls, all under the age of eleven. They live in a small trailer home with only two bedrooms. One bedroom is used by the parents, and the other by the three girls. The living room has a sofa and a bunk bed. Two of the three boys sleep on the bunk bed, and the other sleeps on the couch. They rotate places on a nightly basis so one person doesn't always get the couch. Every morning, they get up and take the bunk bed apart so they will have space to move around in the living room during the day.

"This family was doing okay until the partnership the father was in got into financial trouble. He went from there to a job at the copper mine. It didn't pay a lot, but they were able to survive. A few months ago, they lost their home and had to move into the trailer. Some of the neighbors have tried to help the mother, but she is stubborn and tries to do everything by herself. She doesn't want to be considered someone who needs a handout.

"Just last week, the father gathered his family around him. He wouldn't look at his children, and he could hardly get the words out because he was so choked up with emotion. 'Kids,' he told them, 'I just lost my job at the mine. We're short on funds and, well, Mom and I decided that we will have to put Christmas off this year. This Christmas, our family is going to have Santa leave us a giant Christmas dinner. We won't be able to afford any other presents. Do you guys understand?'"

Jake continued the story. "As I sat in their living room last night, I looked into the eyes of Billy, the little five-year-old boy, and he asked, 'What do you mean we're not going to have a Christmas? I don't understand that, Dad. Did something happen to Santa Claus this year?'

"After giving his death-to-Christmas speech, the father kept away from his children. Since then, he's spent every day looking for a job. So far, he hasn't found one."

Jake looked at his students and paused. Quietly, he asked, "Do you guys want to help this family?"

In unison the students said, "Yeah! We do."

Jake quieted them down and said, "Let's see. Why don't we put Cheyenne and Harrison in charge of this project? Yeah, I want you to run any ideas by them. Now, I know you guys don't have much money, and I don't expect you to worry about having to come up with money to buy expensive things for this family. I want you to think about ways we can make this a real Christmas for them. Think about things you have that you don't use any more, or things you have grown out of. Think of the children and what you would like on Christmas morning if you were in their shoes. I expect this will take more thinking than doing, and we don't have a lot of time, so we need to get busy."

Two days later, when Cheyenne walked into the house after school, Nichole grabbed her hand and said, "Not so fast. We have some shopping to do."

"What?" Cheyenne asked.

"Are you going to the dance tomorrow night?"

"Yes, I am."

"Well, I'll not have you goin' to any dance lookin' like you just got off the farm," Nichole joked.

Cheyenne couldn't believe how many dresses Nichole made her try on. Cheyenne thought Nichole enjoyed it more than she did. The girl helping them liked a sky-blue dress, saying it brought out Cheyenne's eyes and set off her hair. Nichole loved a forest green dress that really showed off Cheyenne's figure. So did Cheyenne. "Looks like the votes are in," she said when she'd decided. "I'll take the green one."

The following evening, Robert knocked on the door and was invited in by Nichole.

"I am Mrs. Lloyd," she said, "and this is my husband, Richard. Robert, we are glad to meet you. What did you say your last name was? You look really nice."

Robert smiled. "It's Larsen." He was obviously nervous.

Cheyenne finally finished primping and came down to greet Robert. When she walked into the room, his eyes opened wide and he smiled. He was shy, but so was she. *This is great,* Cheyenne thought. *Two people who have absolutely no experience in dating. Who's going to lead whom?*

"Robert, is that flower for me? It will look so nice on my dress. Thank you very much."

Robert just stared. Nichole pinned the flower on Cheyenne's dress and whispered in her ear, "He is kind of cute, but I'm afraid he's a bit shell-shocked. I think it's the dress; it's gotta be the dress."

Cheyenne had a wonderful time at the dance. It was the first school dance she had ever attended. Robert was a perfect gentleman and a good dancer as well. Several times, Cheyenne caught Harrison looking at her from across the room. She turned away each time and tried to think of something—anything but him.

Cheyenne didn't realize that so many of her fellow students considered her a friend. In between every dance, someone would come over and talk to her and Robert. Most everyone complimented her. She felt good—maybe even cute. Her small circle was expanding.

Nichole was waiting at the door when Cheyenne got home. Cheyenne was surprised and inquired, "You're still up? Isn't it a little late for you?"

"Here's the deal, Miss Cheyenne. If you think I'm going to toss and turn all night wondering what happened, you're crazy! So tell me all."

After Cheyenne told her about the dance, Nichole said, "I'm so happy for you, Cheyenne."

"And boys are good for . . . mowing the lawn and what else?" Cheyenne teased.

Chapter 7

DECEMBER 2

The Thanksgiving holiday came and went quickly. Thanksgiving vacation was over, leaving only fifteen more days of school before the Christmas break. Cheyenne had never experienced a Thanksgiving around people whom she liked, and who, weird as it seemed, liked her.

Cheyenne, Nichole, and Richard spent Thanksgiving Day at Richard's parents' home, along with a host of other relatives. Nichole's father and mother had gone on a trip to Mexico for the week, so Nichole told Cheyenne she would only have to eat one Thanksgiving meal this year.

"Usually we have to go to my parents' home first and eat lightly, trying to save room for the meal at Richard's parents' home later," she explained. "It seems they both have control issues, or maybe they just like us. It bums them both out if we don't come, and we haven't figured out any other way to solve the problem."

Janna, Richard's mother, was full of life. She dragged Nichole and Cheyenne into the kitchen as soon as they arrived on the pretext of getting them to help prepare the meal. She really wanted some girl time. Besides, the men had already surrounded the TV and were watching a football game. "Nichole," her mother-in-law asked, "will you finish the rolls?"

"Have you ever made dinner rolls, Cheyenne?" Nichole asked.

"Are you kidding? My experience in the kitchen has always been limited to doing dishes and sweeping floors. You know, the glamorous jobs."

Before the rolls were done, Nichole had taught Cheyenne the finer points of making a real mess in the kitchen while having a great time. Janna, who tried to referee, unknowingly ended up with a flour handprint on the back of her blue sweater. She finally sent the two "kids" out of the kitchen. "You two go see if you can entice the men into a game with the kids," she instructed, "instead of sitting there glued to the TV. You're not doing me any good in here anyway."

Cheyenne learned that she wasn't exempt from the good-natured teasing that the Lloyds inflicted upon one another. She felt comfortable and included, even if the family made her blush time and time again. Of course, all day long everyone asked Janna if the flour handprint on her sweater was a new design, complimenting her creativity. Cheyenne enjoyed the whole day. On more than one occasion, Mr. Lloyd said, "I hate to be called Mr. Lloyd, Cheyenne. How about Babe? If that's hard to say, then you can just call me Gramps."

Cheyenne spent the rest of the Thanksgiving weekend doing things with Nichole and Richard—family things. She was surprised by how much she enjoyed just hanging out with them doing simple things like playing Clue, cleaning the house, and even watching football with Richard. Richard, however, learned that he was now outnumbered, and he paid dearly in every game of Charades. Cheyenne had many religious discussions with both Richard and Nichole. Richard was the logical scriptorian, while Nichole taught from the heart. Living had become fun; even getting up in the morning was something to look forward to.

Cheyenne was still afflicted with the little voice in the back of her head that told her all of this was only temporary, that her new world was going to come to a screeching halt. But now she was able to deal with it. She was prepared to accept whatever happened, good or bad, because she had experienced a life she knew was worth living, whatever the risk. She had decided that she was going to become the "go for it girl." She refused to look backward; she was going forward no matter what the price. Cheyenne had decided to point herself toward the light; the dark was too sad and lonely.

Whenever she felt the darkness creeping in, dragging her into the shadows, she found a place where she could be by herself and pray. She had grown accustomed to seeking God's assistance. It came almost naturally to her. And faith in God? Well, she explained it like this to Nichole: "My life has been a series of passageways and doors. One would open and one would close. I never understood that it was the Lord opening and closing all of those doors. I only discovered it when I started reviewing my life in retrospect. It's hard to see while you're living it, but as you look back over the winding path, it becomes apparent. If it hadn't been for God bringing me to you, I would have been one of those girls Judge Wentworth was talking about. But God directed me through those doors and hallways. I was prepared to come to your house, Nichole. Yes, I have lived a hard life, but I have learned many things, including the blessing of having a mother and father. Every day, I thank my God for you, Nichole, and for Richard."

Back in school after the long holiday weekend, Cheyenne tried to balance all of the impending Christmas activities with her schoolwork. She had taken to eating lunch in the seminary room. It was quiet there. She could get some homework done, read the scriptures, or just relax. Jake wasn't usually around, but one day he walked in. Cheyenne knew she wouldn't get any homework done. The thought made her smile.

"Fancy meeting you here, Brother Wolfgramm," Cheyenne teased. "What's the matter? Did you get bored at the U and come here looking for some lost souls to save?"

"No. You see, I have three girls trying to put their hooks in me, and I knew they would never find me here. They think I should go to the Christmas dance and, well, me and dancing just don't mix. Besides, what would you do without me for a day?"

"Jake, I was just thinking about you. I was thinking that it is so quiet around here without you that I might even be able to get some homework done."

Jake pulled up a chair and sat down in front of Cheyenne. "Have you got a minute?" he asked.

"Sure," she answered. "I always have a minute for you. You now have fifty-seven seconds left."

"Cheyenne, let me tell you a story."

"I don't know if you have enough time to tell me one of your stories, seeing as how you only have forty-three seconds left," she joked.

Jake continued, smiling at first and then growing more serious. "The scriptures tell us that the Lord did not light the candle and put it under a bushel," he said, "but on a candlestick, so it would give light to all. Harrison hasn't figured that out yet."

"No! You're joking. You don't mean Mr. GQ," Cheyenne mocked.

"The reason I assigned you and Harrison to work on this Christmas project is that I hoped a little of you would rub off on him. I believe Harrison has been blessed with many talents. But right now, he's having problems seeing anyone's light but his own. I'm not giving up on him; I'm just telling you that I am sorry to have passed one of my problems on to you."

"An apology," replied Cheyenne. "Admit it! You owe me one."

"Okay, okay, I owe you one," Jake admitted. "I guess I really don't have a story, but I do have a problem I hope you can help me with." Jake was serious; Cheyenne could tell by the look on his face.

"I am concerned because it seems that my students all think they have to go out and buy a bunch of presents. That's not what I wanted when we started this project. Have you come up with any ideas to turn the tide since you just happen to be in charge of this project?"

Cheyenne didn't respond immediately. She had been thinking a lot about the assignment. After a moment, she looked Jake in the eye and said, "Jake, for the last six months or so I have lived a dream. I have a home. I've never had somewhere I called home before—never! Everyone in this class has accepted me as is, no questions asked. No one has inquired about my past. The Lloyds, you, and my fellow students have given me a gift I'm not sure I can ever repay. But I want to try. I think I have an idea. I guess it's my chance to say thanks for what everyone has given me, while at the same time trying to provide an example of gift giving. To tell you the truth, I have agonized over telling you about it. I'm fearful, embarrassed, and ashamed."

Jake knew now was not the time to interrupt.

"Jake," she continued, "I have only owned a few things in my life, and almost nothing that really mattered. My most prized possession is this necklace." Cheyenne held up a pendant. "I have worn it every day since Nichole gave it to me. The heart-shaped pendant appears to have been broken and then mended. Nichole said it had a special meaning for her, and that someday, she would tell me the story behind the broken heart.

"She gave it to me shortly after I came to live with her. I treasure it because Nichole gave it to me; it was one of her most prized possessions. To me, it is a symbol that love can mend even a broken heart like it has mine. It reminds me of everything good in my life. Yet, as much as this necklace means to me, I have decided I am going to give it to Jane, the eleven-year-old girl in our family. I am going to write a note telling her what I have learned during the past six months about life and the goodness of people. I want Jane to understand what I've learned about gift giving—that it's not measured by the amount of money you pay for the gift but by the worth of the gift to the giver. Most important, I want her to know that having someone love you can always mend a broken heart. Love is the gift—the ultimate gift."

Cheyenne was silent for a long time, obviously deep in thought. "Jake," she said finally, "you see, the funny thing is that the gift of acceptance you and all of the kids in this class have given me was given without you or them knowing who and what I really am. They don't know I don't have a mother or father or that I was a problem child. They don't know how much time I've spent in detention centers, or that I've changed my life. I'm not the person I used to be. I am a different person, a better person, because of the Lloyds, because of you, and because of each of them.

"So you see, for them to understand the significance of their gift to me, they need to know about the person I was. Now can you understand why I'm apprehensive?"

Jake felt his chest tighten up. He reached over, took her hand, and gave it a little squeeze. "All you need to do is tell them exactly what you just told me. Your story will touch their hearts and give them a real-life example of true gift giving. It's perfect."

Then Jake, rubbing his eyes, said, "Cheyenne, you are a doll! Your story is going to make all the difference in the world."

"Yep, that's me! Someone with a criminal record, whose only gift to give is a little necklace. After I tell the class about my past, I'm sure they will all be lining up to congratulate me."

The next day, Jake tried to get everyone's attention. It was getting harder for the class to pay attention as Christmas approached, but Jake got their attention quickly when he let out a deafening Tongan war yell.

"Now that I have your attention," he said, "today is the first day of our best Christmas ever! As you know, I put Cheyenne and Harrison in charge of our Sub-for-Santa project. I also told everyone our project is not just about buying presents—it's about giving gifts. There is a difference. I want you guys to listen to the story Cheyenne wants to tell you. It may help you understand what I've been trying to tell you. So, without further introduction, I give you our own Cheyenne Carson."

Everyone cheered, whistled, and hollered, including Jake. Not exactly the mood Cheyenne thought appropriate, but Jake always did things his own way. He should have been a cheerleader instead of a football player.

Cheyenne stood with her head held high, her wheat-colored hair covering her shoulders. She tried to look dignified, but she was frightened inside. She scrutinized every student in the class; she tried to look into their eyes. The class fell silent. After several minutes, in a quiet voice, Cheyenne began, "Guys, I have a story to tell you. It's not a pretty story, but it's true. My only hope in telling it is that you will understand my gratitude for what each of you and my family have given me. I am so humbled that, well, I think I need to pass it on—you know, turn around and do something for someone else that is just as good as what you have given me.

"I'm not sure I'm making any sense, but bear with me. I'm getting there. Let me start with you guys. You probably don't even know it, but each of you has given me a gift unlike any I have ever received before."

The class was attentive, and all eyes were turned in her direction. Harrison, she noticed, was particularly attentive.

Cheyenne began, "I was abandoned by my mother when I was still a baby. She left me at 7-Eleven when I was about one. The only thing I know about her is that she didn't know who my father was. From that day until about six months ago, I lived in a bunch of foster homes and juvenile detention centers. You know, I never had a place I called home. I have never had a mother hug me and tell me that things were going to be okay. In short, I have always felt really sorry for myself. I wallowed in self-pity for seventeen years. Now, looking back, I realize that I created most of my own problems. But I felt cheated. I didn't have a family or a home, and the most I ever owned were the clothes on my back and the things I kept in my pockets. I was expected to live in intolerable situations, in foster homes whose families only took me in because they were paid money by the state. I got to the point that if I wanted something, I took it. What was worse is that I didn't feel bad about stealing. I thought everyone owed it to me because they had it and I didn't."

The audience could not believe what they were hearing. Harrison looked shocked. Cheyenne continued. "It was about six months ago that I found the person who will always be my mom. But you know, I've never called her mom before, but that's my mistake and I'm going to change that today. Anyway, the first time I saw her, I was sitting on the witness stand in front of a judge who wanted to put me away permanently. If it hadn't been for Nichole Lloyd, my mom, I would be in jail or a detention center instead of going to this school and standing here. Nichole argued with the judge. She wouldn't give in. No matter how bad he made me sound, she just wouldn't listen. She told him that just because someone's life is broken a little, you don't throw it away. She wanted the chance to help me, and she wanted me to have a chance. Well, the judge gave in. I think he just wanted to get Mrs. Lloyd out of his courtroom. All she has done is love me. She gave me the one gift no one else had ever given me before, the gift of love. Somehow, she healed my broken heart and gave me back my life.

"I still have a long way to go, but I am trying. Every minute of every day brings me new joys and happiness: a happiness I have never felt before, not in my whole life.

"Telling you guys the story of my life is the hardest thing I have ever done. I knew I could ruin everything. You have been great! You treat me like a normal person. But I'm not! All of you, by offering me friendship, have given me a chance. I never asked, and I certainly didn't deserve it. You will never know what it has meant to me to be accepted and cared about. It is the greatest of all gifts, and you didn't even know you were giving it. So now you know who I really am."

Cheyenne tried to catch her breath, which was coming in

gulps. She fought back tears. "I have tried to think of a gift I can give to 'our family' that will matter. I don't have much to give. My most prized possession is this gold necklace." Cheyenne proudly displayed it to the class.

"As you can see, the heart appears to have been broken and then mended. My mom gave it to me soon after I came to live with her. It's mine, all mine. It came to symbolize how love can mend even a broken heart. I have worn it every day since she gave it to me. It is my most valued material possession. As much as this necklace means to me, I am going to give it to Jane, the eleven-year-old girl in 'our family.' I am going to write her a note describing how love can mend even a broken heart. I'm going to tell her that this necklace symbolizes the healing power of love.

"This year I've been taught about gift giving, which, in a large part, I learned from you guys. Your gift of acceptance is a gift that I never deserved. But I thank you because you have helped make my life a living dream. I believe Christmas is about giving love, and true gift giving is not based on the cost of the gift—it's based on the worth you bestow on the gift you give."

There wasn't a sound in the classroom. Cheyenne didn't dare look at anyone because she felt tears running down her cheeks. *Oh, well,* she thought.

"Thank you, Cheyenne," Jake said when she had finished. "I know what it took for you to talk to us today." Turning to the class, he continued, "Cheyenne explained so simply what I have been trying to tell you for three weeks. She taught us about gift giving from the heart, not the pocket. She taught us how a simple gift can make such a difference, even when we don't know it. But mostly, she has taught us about honor, of doing the right things for the right reason no matter what it costs. One of my heroes, Rob Roy, who, by the way, was not Tongan, said:

> *Honor is something no man can give to you!*
> *Honor is something no man can take from you!*
> *Honor is a gift you give to yourself.*

"Cheyenne, today you have given the gift of honor to yourself."

After a moment, Jake regained his composure and continued. "Okay, this is what I'm going to do. Tomorrow I'm going to bring a box and put it here on my desk. It is time we started filling it with presents for our family."

Jake walked to the blackboard and listed all of the information about the family, including ages, clothing sizes, and names. Then he said, "Now listen, here is the deal. What I want you to do is to bring some presents for each of the kids. Now be nice. Don't bring dolls with their heads off or GI Joe's with missing arms. Bring something really nice that is yours that you don't use anymore. If you want to be really nice, then start saving your money and go buy something extra special, but don't just spend money. Give with your heart. Consider what you have been taught today, and go and do likewise."

Cheyenne finally got enough courage to look around the classroom. She could see the excitement. Her fellow students— her friends—really wanted to help this family. They were all talking back and forth, exchanging ideas for the rest of the class period. Cheyenne watched Jake watch his students. He didn't say a word.

Out of the blue, Harrison walked over to Cheyenne's desk. He sat down next to her, talked to her for a minute, and got up and left the classroom. Cheyenne noticed Jake watching the whole time.

Finally, Jake stood up, asked for quiet, and gave the closing prayer. Cheyenne had heard a lot of prayers lately, but the one Jake offered that day sounded as if he was talking directly to Father in Heaven, as if was standing right there. Cheyenne even looked up to check. When he finished, he was choked up. "Okay, you guys," he mumbled, "I'll see you in the morning."

Cheyenne tried to slip out of class quickly. It didn't happen. Small groups and individuals stopped her and said, "Thanks, Cheyenne." She was amazed. No one avoided her; she was still everyone's friend. She didn't know what to say or do, but she knew that these were the greatest kids she had ever met.

Jake was still sitting at his desk after the classroom had emptied. Harrison came back in and sat next to Jake. It was a few minutes before he spoke.

"Jake, I want to apologize. I've been a real jerk and I know it. Let me tell you something. I have never heard anything so simple and so honest. Cheyenne's story really had an impact on me today. I was speechless. I was trying to understand the things she told us. I thought I had my life all figured out when I came to Utah. I knew what I wanted out of life. I knew where I was going. But then this girl, this girl who has almost nothing, explained it to me in a way that has touched my heart."

Harrison was quiet for some time. "I want the feeling, the feeling she had, the one that she told us about."

Jake thought for a moment before he replied. "You're right, Mr. Daniels. Today we were treated to a taste of the Spirit. Just think. Cheyenne, by telling her story, was exposing herself to shame, ridicule, and maybe even the loss of friends. I'm so proud of her. And you know, I thought I was the teacher here."

"Jake, can you wave your magic wand and give me the feeling?"

"I've got an idea, Harrison—something I want you to try. Meet me here tomorrow night at seven and we'll talk about it. There's something I want you to do."

Bright and early the next day, Jake brought an empty box that had contained a case of Wheaties and set it in the front of the room on his desk. Harrison was the first student to arrive that morning; he got there well ahead of everyone else. He walked over to the box and dumped an armload of presents into it, filling it halfway. Jake smiled.

"I may not be able to give anything as valuable as Cheyenne's gift, but I'm going to try to help," Harrison said. "Now, don't tell anyone who brought in these presents, understand?"

Jake nodded and continued to smile.

Cheyenne was the next person to arrive that morning. She was still feeling a little timid, and she didn't quite know how to act. She walked over to the box, took out her one present, which she had wrapped with care, and placed it on top of the other brightly wrapped gifts.

Cheyenne was not really paying much attention to the box. She was distracted by Harrison and Jake, but it suddenly dawned on her that the box was already half full. Cheyenne smiled, looked at Jake, and said, "So there really is a Santa Claus, huh? It looks like he didn't waste any time getting here. Who is to thank for all of these presents?"

Jake just smiled and said, "I guess your little speech worked."

"Come on, Jake, give it up. Who brought in all these gifts?"

Jake just smiled and said, "That's not for me to tell or you to know."

Cheyenne walked back to her seat, never looking at Harrison. She watched as each student came into class. She was amazed and couldn't believe what was happening. Each student brought one, two, or even three presents and put them in the box. It wasn't long before the box was full and students began stacking presents on Jake's desk. Cheyenne's heart pounded. Every student looked her way and smiled at her after putting gifts in the box. Craig Divet walked over and whispered in her ear, loud enough for everyone to hear, "I'm with you, Cheyenne."

It was a miracle. Instead of branding her as an outcast, these kids were now going out of their way to let her know she was okay by them. She could hardly contain her joy, and it almost spilled out in a flood of tears she fought to hold back.

Immediately after the opening prayer, Craig stood up in the back of the room and said, "Jake, I thought you said you were going to bring a box for the presents. You call that a box? Why, it can't even hold the presents we brought in today, and this is only day one. We still have fourteen more to go. Hey, Jake, tomorrow why don't you bring a real box?"

"Yeah," everyone said. "Bring a real box, a big box, Jake."

Jake looked at all of his students, each with a giant smile. Finally he said, "Okay, you guys, tomorrow I'll bring a real box, a big box."

That night, Jake went to several stores until found a big box. It was at least four feet wide and four feet tall. *These kids will never be able to fill this box. They are going to be one surprised group when they see it,* he thought. He was one up on them, he was sure.

Jake got to class early the next morning. Already, stacked in front of the classroom door, was a pile of presents. A note sat on the top of the stack. Jake read it.

"We're not in your class, but we heard about your Sub-for -Santa and wanted to help. Thanks! We loved doing this."

Jake took the presents and placed them, along with those from the Wheaties box, into the big box. He set that box on the floor in front of his desk. He was proud of his effort to find a big box and couldn't wait to see the faces of his students. He chuckled as he thought about them.

When the students came in that morning, they gasped when they saw the box. Craig walked in and exclaimed, "Now that's a box, Jake. Good work!"

Two days later, the new box was overflowing with gifts. Cheyenne was overwhelmed by the generosity of the group. She had noticed Harrison putting presents in the box each morning. He kind of surprised her. It was almost as though he didn't want anyone to see him, and that surprised her even more.

Harrison seemed different. Cheyenne couldn't put her finger on it, but something had changed.

Chapter 8

DECEMBER 9

Nichole was standing at the door when Cheyenne arrived home from school. She had a sly, mischievous look on her face, and Cheyenne knew exactly what that meant. It had happened again. This was the fifth day in a row Nichole had met her at the door holding yet another beautiful white rose in a crystal vase.

Nichole offered the flower to Cheyenne, taunting her a little. "Whoever is sending these must have it really bad! That's five white roses in five days."

"They're pretty, aren't they," Cheyenne remarked.

Cheyenne thought turnabout was fair play, so she asked, "Now, the question is, are the flowers for you or for me?"

Nichole shook her finger at Cheyenne. "You are not going to get off that easily. You and I both know the flowers are for Cheyenne Carson. Richard doesn't seem to know about the flowers, so they can't be for me. As additional evidence on that point, I direct your attention to the hang tags that came with the flowers, which read, 'Cheyenne.'"

"Oh yeah, you would have to remember that," Cheyenne replied.

"It's time for you to fess up, girl. Who keeps sending you flowers?"

Cheyenne shrugged, crossed her heart with her left hand, fingers crossed, and said, "I don't have a clue. Maybe we should hire a handwriting expert to help us."

Nichole brought her hand from behind her back. She was holding a white envelope with Cheyenne's name on the front. "I almost steamed it open today. I have been dying to find out the identity of your mystery man. Not that I don't have my suspicions, though."

Cheyenne held the envelope up to the light, trying to see if it had been tampered with. "I don't see any signs of tampering, but I wouldn't put it past you, not for a second." Cheyenne walked across the living room and sat on the couch, stalling for time. "What if I don't want to know who is sending the flowers? You know, it could destroy the excitement or my dreams if it isn't who I think it is."

Nichole was eager for Cheyenne to open the card. "Don't keep me waiting any longer," she entreated. "Just open the stupid card."

Cheyenne held the card for a minute to aggravate Nichole further. "Okay," Nichole said, "since you brought it up, who would you like it to be from?"

Cheyenne did not want to answer that, so she opened the envelope and pulled out the card. She read it, holding it so Nichole couldn't read it. She closed her eyes as if she were praying, trying to keep a smile off her face and not saying anything for about thirty seconds.

Cheyenne knew Nichole could take only so much. Finally, Nichole said, "Okay, Cheyenne, I've suffered enough. Who is it?"

"The problem is, anything I say will simply be used against me," Cheyenne responded. "So promise me that if I tell you whose name is on this card, you will not tease me for at least ten minutes."

"Come on, Cheyenne, that's not fair."

"I guess we are both out of luck today," Cheyenne said, handing Nichole the card, watching her expression as she read it.

"Darn," Nichole said.

"Tell me what you think it means," Cheyenne said. "Use your telepathic powers."

Nichole read the four printed words out loud: "White is for purity."

Nichole hesitated, thought for a minute, and then said, "Okay, let's try this. These white roses are pure, without any flaws. They symbolize something perfect to whoever is sending them. He's trying to tell you that he thinks you are perfect. Pure! What do you think?"

"Me? If that's the answer, then this guy obviously doesn't know me. He would have to be from the other side of the galaxy not to know about me. We can cross everyone I know off of the who-done-it list. Do you want to try again, contestant number two, or do you pass?"

Nichole sat down on the couch next to Cheyenne and turned to face her. "Cheyenne, let me explain something to you, something you keep missing. The Lord has promised us that when we repent of our sins, he will remember them no more, that we will be as white as the driven snow, or in this case, as white as this beautiful rose. It's what the Atonement is all about. It's what Christ's life was about. It's why we celebrate Christmas. We try to remember his gift to us; his gift of forgiveness and love."

"That's easy for you to say. But it's not so easy for me to believe," Cheyenne replied.

"Cheyenne, you have to be able to forgive yourself, and you aren't doing very well in that department."

"How can I forgive myself?" Cheyenne asked. "I knew what I was doing."

"We all have the same problem, Cheyenne. Each one of us has done things we knew weren't right. The Lord also knew this would happen. He doesn't want us to suffer our whole lives because of our mistakes. All he asks is that we admit our mistakes, feel sorrow for them, and promise never to do them again. The purpose of the Atonement is to take care of all our wrongs. Christ took upon himself the sin. If you don't forgive yourself, you are denying the power and purpose of the Atonement. "

Cheyenne thought for a minute. "I think I understand what you are telling me," she said, "but it is a little more difficult to apply; at least it is for me."

"So much for the lecture. I just want you to know that you're okay in my book, and I don't want you to continue to worry about your past. Start again. Live life to its fullest. Go for it.

"But let's get back to your mystery man," Nichole said, thinking while she was talking. "I think this guy has gone to a lot of trouble. He is really quite original. So tell me, under threat of being denied chocolate for thirty days, who you think it is?"

Cheyenne pretended to think really hard, and then she sighed. "Well, actually, there is this gorgeous hunk in my psychology class who has been drooling over me every day."

"Names, give me names."

"Just kidding. I told you that I have no idea who would send me flowers, especially after my speech in seminary the other day. I didn't think anyone would ever . . . Wait a minute! My speech was six days ago, and the flowers started arriving the next day. There must be a connection."

Nichole thought for a minute and said, "Maybe he's telling you that he doesn't care about who you were before because all he sees now is a beautiful person." She paused, as if she was receiving inspiration. "You don't think it could be . . . no, it couldn't be what's-his-name."

"Don't say it, Nichole. Don't even say his name. I can't stand him. Not even a little bit."

"You're still just a wee bit touchy whenever you-know-who's name comes up, Cheyenne. Out with it. I don't think you are telling me everything."

"Okay, okay, " Cheyenne said, smiling. "The other day, after I finished my speech in seminary, everyone in the classroom started talking. It was mass confusion. Harrison came over to my desk. He looked at me and almost seemed sincere when he said, "Cheyenne, I apologize. Whatever I've done, I'm sorry. I've never met anyone quite like you."

Nichole continued to gaze at Cheyenne. "Okay, truth or dare?" she asked and then grinned.

Cheyenne knew she couldn't choose dare, so she said, "Truth, but this isn't fair."

"Oh, I don't care if it's fair. All I want is the truth. Now, admit you like Harrison just a little."

Cheyenne feigned horror. "Like him? You've got to be kidding! The only reason he is paying any attention to me is because I am the only girl who doesn't give him the time of day. I not only don't like him, I can't stand him! But since I have to tell the truth, he is kind of cute, isn't he?"

They both laughed. Cheyenne continued, "Truth. When he is around, I feel kind of, well, I feel weak in the knees, and it's like I have flutter-bys in my stomach. And I have an issue with my heart because it starts pounding. I used to think it was adrenalin because he irritated me so much; now I think he irritates me in more ways than one."

"I knew it! I knew it!" exclaimed Nichole, as though she had finally discovered something important. "Mr. GQ is the flower guy."

"I don't think you can draw that conclusion," Cheyenne responded. "There's too little evidence to incriminate."

"Don't start getting technical with me, girl," Nichole replied. "He's the one."

Two short days later, the box in Jake's room couldn't hold any more gifts. Cheyenne simply couldn't believe what was happening. Jake got everyone's attention. "Guys, I don't know what to say. Look at all these presents! Our family is going to have the best Christmas ever. I never in my wildest dreams thought you guys could pull this off."

Cheyenne had noticed that Harrison seemed to be smiling a lot more these days. She had also watched him make a trip to the box every day before any of the other students came into the classroom. She began to wonder if he had taken a personal challenge to fill the box all by himself. Then, as if on cue, the class voice, Craig Divet, stood up again. In fact, he stood on his chair and looked Jake straight in the eye. "Jake, I thought you said you were going to get a big box," he said.

With tears in his eyes, Jake looked at all of the bright, smiling faces. Looking back at Jake brought tears to Cheyenne's eyes. All of the students, these kids from the wrong side of the tracks who had very little money, had discovered giving, and they loved it. The Christmas spirit, the desire to give, filled Cheyenne's whole soul. Giving couldn't be a sacrifice. It was a get to, not a have to, and she knew it.

Jake's eyes were beginning to tear, yet he felt the gauntlet being thrown down once again. He smiled, blinked back the tears, and said, "Okay, you guys want a big box? Well, this time I'm going to find a *big box.*"

The whole class roared.

Jake was now caught up in the spirit of the group and became the cheerleader. "Do you guys want me to find a really big box?" he asked.

"Yeah!" everyone responded. "A *big box!*"

Jake raised his arms to quiet the noise. "Okay, tomorrow I'm going to bring the biggest box you have ever seen." *What have I gotten myself into this time?* he wondered.

That night, after finishing one of his finals at the U, Jake borrowed a truck from a friend and began searching for a bigger box. He went to stores all over the city. Store after store told him they didn't have any huge boxes, but Jake would not give up.

Of course, he thought, *I'll try a furniture store!* He drove on with a silent prayer in his heart, soon finding a popular furniture outlet store. Jake went into the store and found the receptionist. He told her about his quest.

"Go talk to Bill in the warehouse out back," she instructed. "Around here, we call him Methuselah because he has been here for almost a hundred years. If there is such a box, he can find it. Be warned, though, he is a little cranky. If you take him a candy bar, he will probably help you out."

Jake found a candy machine and bought the biggest candy bar in it. Then he bought another. *If one's good, two will be even better*, he thought, and he turned and headed out back to find Bill.

Jake recognized Bill from fifty feet away, and even from that distance he looked ornery. He looked old and grouchy, and Jake hadn't even said a word to him yet.

"Hi, I'm Jake," he said, and he stuck out his hand. "I was told by the nice lady inside that if I brought you a candy bar, you might be able to help me solve my problem."

"So what's your problem?" Bill mumbled.

Jake explained the reason he needed a big box, telling Bill that his seminary students kept making him find bigger boxes to hold all the presents they were collecting for a Sub-for-Santa program. "So, Bill," Jake asked, "do you think you can help me?"

Bill chuckled. "Okay," he said, "now that you are through feeding me a story, what is it that you really want?"

"I am looking for the biggest box I can find."

Bill remained skeptical. "Are you serious?" he asked. "You want a really big box?"

"Yeah, I want a really big box!"

"Are you sure you want a *really* big box?"

"You know it, mister!"

"Well, follow me, son," Bill said.

They seemed to be taking the long route, winding around boxes, furniture, and odds and ends that were stacked everywhere. They left the building and went into another—a back warehouse where the store kept another huge inventory. They proceeded through this second warehouse, finally arriving at the back, where they stood facing two huge double doors.

Bill started laughing again. He said, "Before I show you this box, I want to know why your mother named you Rake."

Jake smiled and said, "No, she named me Jake, not Rake." Bill laughed and said, "Well, Flake, the joke's on me. But behind those two doors is the biggest box I have ever seen."

Bill walked over to the wall and flipped on a light switch that turned the lights on in the room behind the two huge doors. It was like a scene from a movie, the light in the backroom filtered through the edges of the doors. "This is some performance," Jake said. "I can't wait to see what you've got behind those doors."

Bill walked over to the doors and pushed them open. Behind them was the biggest box Jake had ever seen. It was over six feet deep, eight feet long, and at least six feet high. Jake turned to Bill and asked, "Where in the world did you get such a big box?"

Bill was enjoying himself, and he didn't seem to be as ornery as the lady had said. "Well, there was this farmer from Tooele who ordered this custom-built, super double-door refrigerator, and this is the box it came in. It was so big that I didn't have the heart to throw it away. If you want this box to hold the presents for your Sub-for-Santa, I will let you have it."

"I want that box!" Jake said. "I couldn't even imagine a box this big. I have never seen a bigger one in my whole life."

Bill came back with a forklift to move the box from the warehouse out to Jake's truck. Bill helped Jake cut the box so it would fit in the bed of the pickup.

"How are you going to get this thing off the truck and into your classroom?" Bill asked.

Jake laughed. "Hey, man, I'm a football player. I can do anything." Bill laughed again and wished Jake luck. "Let me know how your little project and the big box work out, okay, Flake?"

By the time Jake got back to the seminary building with the box, it was nearly one in the morning. Jake struggled to get it into his classroom. Then he had to reassemble the box. When he had finished, he put the box in the middle of the room and moved the chairs to form a circle around it. Jake found a small stepladder, which he placed next to the box so the students could climb up to put their presents inside.

When he finally finished and drove home, it was four in the morning. He went to bed and slept for an hour. Then he had to rush back to school before the kids started to arrive. He was dead tired, but he wasn't going to miss the looks on his students' faces when they walked through the door. They had challenged him, and he had met their challenge.

Chapter 9

DECEMBER 12

Day after day they came, one white rose in a glass vase. No one had ever given Cheyenne flowers. Neither Nichole nor Cheyenne knew for sure who the secret suitor was, but they both had their own ideas. Hoping to stir up some discussion on the subject, Nichole teased Cheyenne. "It has to be Robert," she said.

"What? What do you mean?" Cheyenne asked.

"You know, the timid flower giver," Nichole replied.

"No, it's not him. It's the guy I don't ever want to talk about."

"Let's see," Nichole said. "I think I'm going to add Mr. GQ to the list of people you don't want to admit that you like; but if you do like them, you don't want them to know you like them. That is, if you ever admit to yourself that you like them. But other than that, I think you're just having another blonde day."

"What? Oh it just seems lately that I'm never sure what I think or feel. Besides, why would some guy send me flowers every day and then not have enough guts to admit or even to take credit for it? I mean, what's the point?"

Nichole grinned. "Well, I imagine Mr. GQ knows that if he

tells you he's sending you flowers, you will probably dump them on his new car."

"I wouldn't! Would I?"

Later that evening, Nichole walked into Cheyenne's room. Cheyenne was looking at the arrangement of flowers and vases on her nightstand. "Cheyenne, some of those roses are starting to look a little haggard," Nichole said.

"I know. But it's hard to just throw them away. What do you do with old flowers anyway? Keep them in a scrapbook or something? I hate to just dump them."

"I guess you could dry one to save. You know, for posterity. Otherwise, you put them in the trash," Nichole replied.

Cheyenne started to gather up the shabby flowers. She put one in a large dictionary and dumped the rest in the garbage. Cheyenne looked at all the vases. Her gaze lingered on the latest rose, still sitting on her dresser. *The sole survivor*, she thought. She wasn't sure why, but she liked getting flowers. Yes, they were beautiful, but all of the attention felt awkward. Maybe she was just uncomfortable with knowing that someone cared. *Why would someone bother sending flowers and then keep it a secret?* she wondered. It bothered her. In fact, a lot of things seemed to annoy her lately. In the past, she had always prided herself on being able to control her feelings. Now she felt totally out of control. On one hand, she loved the flowers, but at the same time, she thought she hated the fact that they might be from Harrison.

Cheyenne saw Nichole watching her, and Nichole started laughing. She couldn't stop laughing. Cheyenne knew it was something she had done, but she didn't know what. So she looked at Nichole, waiting for her to stop. Finally, Nichole said, "Cheyenne, I wasn't laughing at you, not entirely. I was just remembering. It's funny when you look at it from this side. I'm sorry. You are all girl, all emotion, and you don't know how to deal with it. I can remember feeling exactly what you are feeling—

hormones, panic, temporary insanity—who knows? But don't worry, we have all gone through it. It doesn't help to try to figure it out because it doesn't figure. However, I give you about a 75 percent chance of recovery."

"Medication. There must be something to help," Cheyenne said. "My stomach and heart just can't seem to relax."

"Cheyenne, I see you started a journal," Nichole observed. "Try to tell your journal exactly how you feel and why, even if you don't know. It will make great reading material in a few years. You might even get a few laughs."

Nichole walked into the living room and jumped on Richard's lap, wrapping both arms around his neck. She kissed him and turned off the basketball game he was watching. Cheyenne sat on her bed, listening to Richard and Nichole talk.

"Richard, I don't know when I've been so happy. Is it possible that it was just five months ago that I brought home an introverted, backward, withdrawn, skittish young woman? Look at her now! She's so beautiful—so precious. She fought it each step of the way. She wanted this new life but was hesitant, wondering if she really belonged, if she deserved it, and if it was only temporary like everything else in her life. I keep wanting to scream at her 'Trust us. Trust yourself! You'll be okay. You can do it.'"

Richard kissed her and said, "It's all because of you, Nichole. You have been to her what she never had: a mother, a friend, someone who simply cared. She has turned out to be a wonderful young lady, although I can say there were times I questioned your inspiration."

"I never had a doubt," said Nichole. "I knew she was meant to be my daughter from the beginning."

Richard looked into Nichole's eyes. "You know, I think Cheyenne is just about as important to you as you have been to her. I like to see the sparkle back in your eyes. It hasn't been there for a long time."

How could I be so lucky? Cheyenne thought as she got in bed and snuggled under the covers. As she closed her eyes, she remembered Nichole telling her never to be afraid to dream. She

111

wanted to say, "Nichole, I am living a dream and I don't even need to close my eyes."

When Cheyenne awoke early the next morning, she thought, *Why early again? I have always been able to sleep until noon.* As she tossed and turned, she began to form some ideas, make plans, and develop a course of action. Maybe she could start today and not have to wait until tomorrow.

Cheyenne arrived at seminary early Monday morning. Jake hadn't arrived, but Harrison was reading his scriptures. *Well, there's no time like the present. Don't back out now,* Cheyenne told herself. She clenched her fists like she was getting ready to fight and walked toward his desk. He looked up from his book as Cheyenne crossed the room, watching her every step of the way. *Darn,* she thought. *Why does he have to look at me like that? And why do I have to get flustered?*

When Cheyenne stopped, he smiled and said, "I'll bet you've come to accept my dinner invitation, right?" His tone was milder and more humble than it had been before.

"Yes! I mean no. I mean, I don't know. But I would like to know why."

"Why what? I'm just sitting here reading my scriptures, watching a beautiful girl walk over to talk to me. Whatever you think I did this time, it wasn't me. I promise."

Cheyenne tried to ignore his presence, his question, but mostly his eyes. She tried to remember what she was doing and what she wanted to say. *Get a grip,* she said to herself.

"Why are you sending me flowers every day?" she asked.

"Me?" Harrison asked, pointing to himself. "Why on earth would you think I was sending you flowers? Not that it's a bad idea."

Jake walked in and joined the conversation without asking permission. "Cheyenne, did you say that Harrison is sending you flowers every day?" he asked. "Now, Harrison, I think that's a perfectly charming way to treat a young lady. Good show, my man. What's the matter, don't you like flowers, Cheyenne?"

"Ah, boys," Cheyenne sighed as she walked over to her seat. *Do they ever grow up to be men?* She was flustered, although she wasn't sure why. Jake turned and said to Harrison, "Don't give up on her. She's a keeper."

I really let him know how I feel, didn't I? So much for all those resolutions I made this morning, Cheyenne thought.

She was so wrapped up in her thoughts that she had not even noticed the new addition to the room. Eventually her eyes fell upon it. There it was, the biggest box she had ever seen—a box nearly six feet high and almost as wide, and eight feet long. Cheyenne shook her head, smiled, and looked at Jake who had a smug look on his face. He watched the expression of every student who walked into the classroom. She could tell he loved every minute.

Craig finally walked into the room. He whistled, and a big smile crept across his face. He stopped dead in his tracks and loudly and enthusiastically said, "Now that's a box! That's a big box. It's huge!"

Everyone agreed, and the underlying buzz of excitement and comments about the box continued. Jake was obviously enjoying every minute of his triumph. "Checkmate," he said to the class.

Craig returned the barb. "Remember, Jake, the game's not over until it's over. We still have eleven days and a few more moves. It might be check but not checkmate."

Jake held up his hands. "Hey, guys, I was just giving you a hard time. You have already surpassed my wildest dreams. With the presents we now have, our family is going to have the best Christmas ever. You don't have to do any more."

"Jake," Craig replied, "you ain't seen nothin' yet."

"It's 'anything,' Divet."

"Let me tell you a story," Jake said.

The students groaned.

"You see, I had this plan to tell you a different Christmas story every day, hoping you would get really excited and motivated about the Sub-for-Santa project and Christmas. But you know, the stories no longer seem important. It seems to me that I'm not teaching you guys a thing, it's you who are teaching me."

"Hey, Jake, don't go getting soft on us," Craig called out. "By the way, I haven't seen you put a present in the box yet. What's the deal?"

"Well, now that you've asked, I guess I do have a story to tell you."

"Oh great!" someone said, and everyone laughed.

"You see," Jake began, "when they asked me to teach this class, I was told you guys were the at-risk kids, the ones no one else wanted in their classes. You were the ones that got kicked out or were not invited to take seminary during the day. I thought I was going to have to beat some knobs on your heads just to keep you in line.

"They asked me to teach this class because they thought I could do just that—beat some knobs on your heads, if it became necessary. They knew I wasn't a great teacher, but they thought I was a good enforcer. In fact, Brother Forester didn't ask me to teach this class, he made me. He called in all of his chips. He told me it was payback time. You see, I was worse than the whole group of you combined when I was at Granite. He told me I could relate to you knuckleheads.

"So I came here to try to teach you guys a thing or two. Boy, was I wrong. You intuitively seem to understand the things of the heart—what's right and wrong. You guys are the most likeable 'bad guys' I have ever met."

At the end of class, Jake grabbed Cheyenne's arm. "There are a few things I need to talk to you about. Can you meet me here after school? It'll only take a minute."

"Sure," Cheyenne said. "No problem. But you've never taken just a minute to do anything."

Jake ignored her comment and said, "See you right after school."

Cheyenne listened to her friends' conversations as they walked out of class. The only thing anyone was talking about was the box. It was truly amazing.

All day long, in every one of her classes, someone was talking about the box. It seemed that the whole school had caught on and wanted to see it. All day long, students went past Jake's room just to get a glimpse of the big box. "Now that's a big box!" they would usually exclaim.

The box story didn't stop with the students and their friends. Everyone told their family, and word spread throughout the school community.

After school, Cheyenne strolled over to the seminary building and found Jake sitting with his feet propped up on his desk. He looked at Cheyenne and said softly, "Cheyenne, I am very proud of you."

He always knew how to throw her off guard. She blushed. "Me? What have I done now?"

"Cheyenne, if you only knew. But I guess that's what makes you so special. Don't ever change. And one more thing, never forget that I think you're fantastic."

Cheyenne nodded.

"But to get to the point, I have a story to tell you," Jake continued. "One you haven't heard because I have been sworn to secrecy. However, I'm gonna break my promise, which I usually don't do. Besides, some secrets need to be told. This story is about Harrison. Now hang on. Wait a minute until you go and get all huffy. Hear me out. Promise you will listen to the whole story, okay?"

Cheyenne looked at Jake. "Did he put you up to this?"

Jake smiled. "No. In fact, I promised him I would never tell anyone. He's not as big a jerk as you think he is. Like you, he has made some changes in his life. And so the question is, why do I think it is important I tell you?"

"Yeah, Jake, why do you want to tell me?"

"Because if I were Harrison, I would want the best-looking girl in the school to know I'm not the self-centered jerk she thinks I am."

Cheyenne blushed and responded, "I'll take that as a compliment. Thank you. But I can't promise I will let you get through the story. Let's just say I will try, even if I have to bite my tongue."

"Cheyenne, you will never know the impact your speech, your confession, had on some of your fellow class members. Anyway, something you said got to Harrison. That night, he didn't sleep much, and he did some real soul-searching. The next day, he came in to talk to me. He said, 'Jake, you know I can buy just about anything I want, and yet I'm not happy. I don't have that feeling Cheyenne talked about. Can you imagine going through what Cheyenne has experienced and standing in front of the class, telling us how grateful she was for her life?'" He wanted to feel what you were feeling.

"So I said to Harrison, 'I can tell you how to solve your problem, but telling you won't work. You've been told before. Instead, I want to put this conversation on hold for two weeks. During the next two weeks, I want you to go to Primary Children's Hospital every night and read to the kids. I'll call and make the arrangements. All you have to do is go.'

"Well, I'll be darned if he didn't go for two full weeks, and would you believe he is still going? It's those kids—they'll do it to you every time. One deaf kid told him, 'I'm not handicapped, I just can't hear.' The kids just warmed his heart. Suddenly, number one didn't matter as much. Service is an amazing thing; you forget yourself and start caring about others. Well, it happened to Harrison. The director at the hospital told me the kids are in love with the guy. The director doesn't know who looks forward to the visits more, the kids or Harrison."

Jake paused.

"Well, that doesn't sound anything like the Mr. GQ, I mean the Harrison, I know," Cheyenne said meekly.

"He admitted to me that he knows he doesn't have it all

figured out yet, but he's trying," Jake continued. "He not only continues to go to the hospital, but he has also reached out in other ways. He has committed his efforts to help our family, but he wants his gifts and his service to remain a secret. He thinks it will matter more to him if no one knows. He wants to do it for himself, not for anyone else."

"I've seen him bring in his packages every day," Cheyenne said.

"It's funny," Jake replied, "because each present he brings is individually chosen, and he even wraps all of them himself. Of course, it's not hard to tell which ones he wraps—my little sister could do a better job."

Jake looked into her eyes. He was quiet for some time. Then he said softly, "It was the things you said that made him want to change."

Cheyenne nodded, holding back her emotions.

"I'll tell you, Cheyenne. A miracle happened. I've always thought it's a miracle when people change their beliefs, their habits, the way they think and act. Do you understand what I am trying to tell you?"

"I think so."

"Do you, Cheyenne? You have been a wonderful example of giving. But you still have some issues. You are afraid to open your heart and trust. You keep your feelings locked up in a safe place and refuse to admit even to yourself what or where they are. You've tried to hide from your feelings for a long time, haven't you, Cheyenne?"

Cheyenne was silent. She felt confused and happy and was reeling in turmoil.

"I only have one thing to tell you, Cheyenne. Don't fear. Fear makes us lose before we even start the race. Oh, I almost forgot. There is one more thing I would like to ask you to do, Cheyenne."

Cheyenne stopped him. "Wait a minute," she said. "You said you only had one thing, and now you want to add another."

"Just give him a chance, Cheyenne. You've treated him like

dirt since the day he knocked you down and scattered your books all over the grass. Besides, I think he kinda likes you."

Whispering, and with a voice filled with emotion, she said, "No. No one like him could like me. Not me. Who am I?"

"Cheyenne, don't ever forget this. You are a child of God and he loves you and wants you to be happy. I don't think it was just by chance you came to live with the Lloyds. I think God had a hand in it. Do you know the joy you have brought to the Lloyds, specifically Nichole? She loves you as if you were her own daughter. That's to say nothing about the impact you have made on our class."

"You're nice, Jake. Wait a sec. What did I say? I take it back. You are only nice sometimes."

"Cheyenne, none of it's going away; we're not going away, Nichole's not going away, and neither are you. You can have it all. It's yours for the taking. We all love you, and besides, we wouldn't let you go, even if you tried to."

Cheyenne left Jake's classroom that day feeling thankful for the people who cared about her. She knew there were people who actually loved her. But her feelings for Harrison were even more confused. Maybe she didn't know as much about him as she thought she did. But she still wanted to know why he wouldn't admit to giving her the flowers.

The next two days were unbelievable. Kids, parents, and lots of other people came to the classroom, not just to see the box but also to climb the little ladder and place their packages into it. The box began to fill up, and it seemed there was a different spirit around the school. Cheyenne felt it; it was real. Not one student walked into the room without bringing another package. It was humbling. Chills ran up and down Cheyenne's spine every day. She loved the feeling. She loved Christmas.

Each day, Jake would just shake his head as the packages in the box continued to increase in number.

Cheyenne was excited to tell Nichole about the box and the new presents, but she mostly wanted to talk to her about Harrison. She just didn't know how to bring it up. But she couldn't hide anything from Nichole anyway.

Nichole was not waiting for her at the door. That could only mean one thing: no flower. For some reason, that made Cheyenne upset. Or was it disappointment she felt? Cheyenne walked in and saw Nichole sitting in the kitchen. "What, no flower today?" she asked.

"Oh, there's a flower, for sure. See for yourself. It's on the counter right over there, and it has another card. Maybe we can finally end all our speculation," Nichole said.

Cheyenne saw the vase and flower; encircling the vase was a necklace with a beautiful white pearl pendant. Cheyenne felt like crying. "It's beautiful," she said to no one in particular.

Nichole didn't tease her tonight, but she watched Cheyenne carefully. Cheyenne took the card, sat down at the kitchen bar next to Nichole, and opened it so they could both read it at the same time. Inside was a verse from the book of Matthew, slightly reworded:

"When he had found one pearl of great worth, he went and sold all that he had, and bought it."

A tear ran down Cheyenne's cheek; she couldn't help it. Today had just been too emotional. She removed the necklace from the vase and fastened it around her neck.

"Drats. It doesn't say who it's from," Nichole said, interrupting her thoughts.

"It's from Mr. GQ," Cheyenne said.

"How do you know that?"

"I just know it," Cheyenne replied. "Do you really think it is possible for someone like him to like someone like me?"

Nichole hugged Cheyenne and said, "Have you looked in the mirror lately, young lady? You didn't get nominated for Queen of the Winter Formal because they think you are smart."

"I think you bought them off," Cheyenne teased, quietly adding, "but what if he finds out who I really am?"

119

Nichole looked at Cheyenne. "Then he will like you even more."

Nichole grabbed her hand and pulled her over to the couch. "Come and sit with me. There are so many things I want to tell you."

Nichole talked to her for over an hour.

"Tell me how well you know Jake," Cheyenne asked. "You two seem to go back a long way."

"My younger sister had a crush on him for over three years. They were the same age and dated for a while. I understand he was going down the street to disaster until Brother Forester got hold of him. He made a major change in his life during his sophomore year in high school. After he got turned around, it was 'Johnny, bar the door.' He turned out to be a superstar.

"He is so cool. He's such a good athlete and so good looking. Most Polynesians are content just to be jocks. Others run in gangs. He wanted to be a serious student, although school didn't come easy for him. He had to work hard, but he refused to quit. He wanted to make something of himself. We became the best of friends, and I was actually closer to him than I was to my own brother. He knows things about me that few people know."

Almost immediately, Cheyenne asked, "You mean he can tell me things about you that no one else knows?"

"If he does, I will kill him," Nichole replied.

Chapter 10

DECEMBER 22

Jake was holding an after-school stomp in the seminary room the next day to celebrate the end up of the Sub-for-Santa project. Everyone was invited. For Cheyenne, the day was to be a culmination of many dreams, a day she never thought she would be a part of. She was in high spirits and looked forward to the party with anticipation.

After dinner, Nichole said, "Richard, why don't you go watch a football game or something? We need to do some girl things for a minute, okay?" He shrugged and moved into the front room, pausing to say, "Cheyenne, remember whose side you're on because whenever she starts throwing out phrases like 'girl things,' I know it has to do with spending money."

"Don't pay him any mind, Cheyenne," Nichole interjected. "He knows what's important. And if it costs a little money, so what?"

Cheyenne loved the way they teased each other. She shrugged her shoulders at Richard and said, "What can I do? Besides, I think she carries the swing vote around here anyway."

"I know that only too well," he replied, turning on the TV.

Cheyenne followed Nichole into her bedroom. She lifted a simple, fashionable somewhat trendy red dress off her chair. "I love your dress," Cheyenne remarked. "You'll look dazzling in it. It's beautiful."

"Thank you. That's what I thought too, but the dress is for you. I bought it so you will have something new and Christmasy to wear tomorrow. Maybe even Mr. GQ will take notice," Nichole said.

"You bought this dress for me? Nichole, how will I ever be able to repay you for all you have done for me? You can't keep spending so much money on me. But I do love the dress."

Without any warning, Cheyenne gave Nichole a big hug that said it all. They were both crying. Cheyenne wondered what to say to the person who had given her a life. She so wanted to thank Nichole. She wanted Nichole to be a part of her life forever. She didn't want her to ever go away and was starting to believe she wouldn't. She felt so safe and so loved that her heart was ready to burst.

Finally Cheyenne was able to speak. "Nichole," she said, "you are to me the mother I never had. These last six months I have felt like I was a real daughter, like I was someone special. I have never been loved by anyone before you. I still have nightmares that none of this is real. I don't want to lose you, ever. Every day I thank my Father in Heaven for you. The word 'mother' will forever have only one meaning for me, and that is you. I love you, Mom."

Nichole wouldn't let go of her. Cheyenne had never in her life felt so overcome with emotion. She wondered why. *How was it possible?* The questions didn't seem to matter anymore, though, because she had a mom.

Cheyenne wiped her face, and Nichole handed her the dress. "Cheyenne," she said, "I've always wanted a daughter just like you. Now go try on your dress before I ruin all my makeup." As Cheyenne turned to leave Nichole's room, Nichole said, almost reverently, "Cheyenne, you will never know the gift that you have given me this Christmas."

Where had the time gone? Cheyenne thought back over the past several weeks. One word came to mind: hectic. Tests, parties, Christmas, friends, and school all packed into what seemed like ever-shorter days. Besides, all the dreams and feelings she had shoved into the closet for the past seventeen years were trying to get out, and all at the same time. She just didn't have time to deal with them all.

Cheyenne's life now was full from morning to night, although she still believed seminary started during the night, before morning even had a chance. Before she had come to the Lloyd home, her life had been empty. She didn't have to worry about friends, grades, or, for that matter, boys. It had been a cold, lonely life. She didn't want to go back to it, ever! It seemed like so long ago.

Her thoughts turned to Harrison. They often did lately. For a while it seemed that he had been pursuing her. Now he didn't talk to her or even acknowledge her presence. But he was sending the flowers, wasn't he? Her doubts took over, and she knew that no one like him would ever have anything to do with her. Maybe she had just been a novelty. She knew she really didn't fit into his world. In spite of herself, each time she was around him, her stomach started doing flip-flops and her hands started sweating; she was barely able to carry on a simple conversation.

She tried to rid her head of any thoughts of Harrison, but Jake had told her never to quit the race before it started. Nichole had told her to dream dreams. As good as her life was, it had become a lot more complicated. She knew that for sure. She also knew she was not about to roll up the sidewalk and hang out the closed sign.

Cheyenne still received a single white rose every day. She had not interrogated Harrison any further since she had previously made such a fool of herself. But no one at Granite other than

Harrison could afford to send a flower every day. Why hadn't he admitted to being the gift giver? And why was he completely avoiding her? He made sure they were never alone together. Oh, he was polite, but he did not act like she was alive—and just when she was thinking she might be able to tolerate him. Maybe he wasn't the one giving her the flowers after all.

It had been ten days since the Winter Formal. Cheyenne had been asked to the dance by two boys. She ended up going with Tom James. He was good looking. She met him in her psychology class. The dance had been wonderful, and Tom had been a perfect gentleman. Since the dance, Tom had taken Cheyenne to dinner twice, and she often found him waiting for her after classes to walk her to her next class.

Nichole had asked Cheyenne more than once what had happened to Mr. GQ. Cheyenne admitted she had no idea, but she felt that he had finally figured out that she was not in his league. Tom had come by the house one evening and had spent time getting to know Richard and Nichole. Cheyenne admitted he was fun to have around, and there was no pressure—none at all. He was a good friend. Her stomach behaved when he was around, and she never got sweaty palms. She hadn't yet decided whether that was good or bad.

She continued to battle her emotions. At times she wanted to walk over to Harrison and say, "Okay, when are we going to dinner, and what time do I have to be ready?" but she knew she would never actually be so bold. She didn't know what to do, but she wished she could stop thinking about him.

And yet the flowers and cards continued to arrive. *Was Harrison really sending them and why?* Cheyenne wondered.

The next morning, Cheyenne awoke before her alarm went off. She was eager for the day to begin. She showered and took the time to make sure she looked the best she could. Then she put on the trendy red dress. She looked in the mirror for the hundredth time and decided she couldn't do anything more. She struck a few poses, sighed, and said, "Oh, well. I am what I am."

She had heard that Tom was going to go to the after-school dance in Jake's classroom. She expected Harrison to be there also. She just didn't know what she wanted.

Cheyenne opened the door to her room and saw both Richard and Nichole sitting at the table. Richard stood up and motioned to Cheyenne. He pulled out a chair and made a grand sweeping gesture for her to sit. He said to Nichole, "I don't know if I should let you send her to school looking that good."

Cheyenne smiled. "It's a nice dress. Nichole bought it for me. Whoops, I can't tell you—it's one of those girl things. But I think she used your credit card. So I guess you bought it. Thanks, Richard."

"She did, huh? Well, I guess it's a small price to pay to have such a doll living in our home," Richard replied.

Cheyenne tried to make it a joke, but it didn't work. "Not you too! You guys—what can I say?"

"Cheyenne, don't say anything. Just don't give out your phone number to any boys today. If you do, our phone will ring off the hook the whole holiday season," Richard responded.

Nichole, who had been quiet, said, "No, Cheyenne, it's not the dress. That's just the packaging. It's what's inside that's beautiful. But here's the deal. I want to hear everything that happens today, promise? If not, I'm going to have to go to school with you."

"I promise," Cheyenne answered, holding up crossed fingers on both hands and winking. She finished her breakfast even though she wasn't hungry. Before she left the house, she turned and yelled, "See you later, Mom. And you too, Dad—I mean, Richard." She wasn't quite up to calling him Dad—not yet.

It was amazing how good it made her feel to say those words, but she didn't dare look back at Nichole because she knew Nichole would be loving it just as much as she did.

Cheyenne walked into the seminary class and wondered why everyone else was also early. She felt so good, and everyone seemed to have a smile or something nice to say to her. She glanced at Harrison, and yes, he was also smiling and looking at her. The old knot in her stomach started to twist.

Then, from the back of the room, Cheyenne heard Craig's voice. "Hey, Cheyenne," he yelled, "remember you promised to save the last dance for me tonight; and don't worry, I'll take you home afterward."

Cheyenne blushed. Everybody laughed and someone said, "Fat chance, Divet."

Cheyenne looked at Harrison again. He was still watching her. *Why is he looking at me?* she thought.

Jake also smiled at Cheyenne, and she knew he wanted to make some inflammatory comment about her dress, so she mouthed, "Don't do it, Jake."

He tried to look offended and asked, "Me?"

"Yeah, you!" she responded.

"Just as soon as we get the pretty lady in red to finish the roll," Jake began, "we can get started."

Cheyenne knew her face was close to matching the color of her dress. She wondered if Harrison was looking at her. She wasn't going to look, not while her face was bright red. She gave Jake an "I'm gonna kill you" look, but he just grinned.

Cheyenne's attention turned to the big box. It now looked like a giant pile of Christmas packages. Not only was the box full, but there were also gifts stacked all around it. She was glad to have been a part of it all. She knew that somewhere in the giant stack of gifts was her small, simple present. She hoped it wouldn't get lost in the shuffle. It wasn't much of a gift, but it meant a lot to her.

"I am so proud of you guys," Jake said. "Our family will have to get a room addition just to hold all the presents they are going to get. Can you imagine the looks on their faces when they see this pile of presents?"

The room was filled with excitement. Jake continued, "You

know, I have been waiting for Divet to stand up again in the back of the room and say, 'Jake I thought you were going to get a big box.' Thankfully, he hasn't. I don't think they make 'em any bigger than this one.

"I need to get a couple of you guys to volunteer to help me take these packages over to our family on Christmas Eve," he continued. "I understand most of you will want to be with your families and not out delivering packages. But I need a little help."

Someone shouted from the back of the room, "What did you say?"

Craig, the designated spokesman, stood up and said, "Jake, I don't think you get it. I don't think there's a person in this room who is going to miss this one. I don't think you could keep any of us away even if you tried. Now don't you go and worry 'cause on Christmas Eve we'll be here. Just make sure you make it, and how about being on time for once? We're not in Tonga, you know."

Jake smiled and said, "Okay, now that we've got that settled, we need to figure out Santa's arrival time."

From the back of the room, Craig yelled, "Midnight!" Everyone else agreed.

Jake smiled, "All right, we go at midnight. Are you sure you will be up that late? You know, Santa might not come to your house if he sees you are still up."

"Don't you worry about us, Jake. You just make sure someone wakes you up since we know you won't have a date," Craig retorted.

"Okay then, here's the deal. I will meet you here on Thursday night at 11:30. All of you have to bring a note from your parents telling me that it is okay for you to be out that late."

"A note?" Craig asked. "You've got to be kidding! We're seniors! We don't need a note from our parents. Besides, they'll already be in bed."

Jake chuckled and asked once more, "You sure all you guys want to go?"

"One more time and we're goin' to get rid of you, Jake," Craig threatened.

Tom was standing outside the seminary door waiting for Cheyenne when she came out of class. She glanced back to see Harrison watching her as Tom took her arm. The rest of the day, she noticed that she received more than her share of attention from the boys at school. She had to admit it was fun, but she was surprised by all of it. Maybe Richard had been right—it had to be the dress.

The day flew by. The after-school party and dance was held in Jake's classroom, which, with the big box, had become *the* spot. When Cheyenne arrived, the room was full of students, and Christmas music was playing softly. The box was in the center of the room and the dance was in full swing.

Everyone seemed to be wondering the same thing. "How are we going to get all the presents to the family without getting caught?" Craig asked. "Hey, if Santa can do it, we shouldn't have any problem, right?"

"So when's it gonna happen?" someone asked.

"Midnight," Craig replied. "Jake, turn that music up!"

Cheyenne couldn't believe what was happening to her. She danced with everyone—everyone, that is, except for Harrison. She hadn't sat out a single dance. Even Craig had claimed his dance. "You're still going home with me, aren't you?" he asked. Cheyenne laughed and said, "Only if I don't get a better offer." She was thoroughly enjoying herself, but she kept looking around for Harrison.

Several dances later, Craig yelled at Cheyenne from across the room, "Don't forget. You promised me the last dance."

"Divet, get a life," someone yelled.

"She's going home with me!" someone else said.

Students laughed and one added, "Fat chance you've got, Divet."

Suddenly, Harrison was standing right in front of her, so close that she could touch him. She suddenly forgot how to breathe. He took her hand and they began dancing. With a puzzled expression she asked, "What if I had already promised this dance to someone else?" He didn't reply but kept looking into her eyes. She tried to quiet the pounding of her heart. "Did I miss something, or did you ask me if I would like to dance with you?" she quipped.

"If I would have asked, you probably would have told me no," he replied.

"What gives you that idea?" she asked.

"I don't know, but I've been watching this beautiful blonde dance with every boy in the class. I was dying to meet her, but I didn't ask her to dance for fear of rejection. By the way, what did you say your name was?"

"Oh, I'm that shy girl who sits in her seat wishing every day that Mr. GQ would notice her, talk to her, or even take her out."

His eyes were deep green, speckled with silver. They seemed so strong, yet soft; she hadn't noticed this before. She wiped her clammy hand on the back of her dress. She didn't want him to know she was sweating. They didn't speak as they spiraled around the dance floor. Cheyenne was glad because she wasn't sure she could form an articulate sentence just then. Finally, she just relaxed, stopped thinking, and started enjoying herself. The wall was down, and the pieces were going to fall where they may.

It was then that she realized that she liked having his arm around her. It felt good, but it made her fuzzy headed. So she kept her mouth closed and just looked into his eyes. She hoped he could see more than a blank stare. She leaned in closer and rested her head against his neck. He smelled good. She thought she heard him whisper something.

"What? Did you say something?" Then she heard him say it again. Chills ran up and down her spine, and she shuddered a little. "Cheyenne," he had said, "you are beautiful!"

She moved back and looked into his eyes again, but this time she felt a little more prepared to deal with them. She smiled and asked, "Truth or dare?"

"What?"

"Truth or dare?" she repeated.

"That's a kid's game," Harrison answered.

"Truth or dare?" she demanded.

"All right. Truth!' Harrison replied.

"Why did you ask me to dance today? I mean, you haven't said a word to me in two weeks, and then out of the blue, you think I should dance with you as if nothing had ever happened. I thought that after I made my little confession that you would know the real me and . . ."

Harrison interrupted her. "Are you going to prattle on all day, or are you going to let me answer your first question? I said 'truth,' remember? So it's my turn to respond."

"Oh," she said.

His eyes seemed to come alive with the question. A sly smile appeared on his lips. He was about to speak when Cheyenne put her finger to his lips and said, "Remember you said 'truth.'"

When she removed her finger, he smiled. "Okay. The truth is that Jake made me ask you to dance."

Cheyenne poked him in the ribs and he faked a serious injury. After he quit staggering around, he said, "Cheyenne, you just don't get it. Maybe that's what makes you so beautiful. Remember you told us about the person you were? I don't know that person. I only know the person you are. The person you are now—a budding white rose."

Tears came to her eyes, and she looked down to blink them away.

"You still haven't answered my question," she said softly.

Harrison pressed her a little closer and said, "I remember a parable from the New Testament that goes something like this, 'Who, when he had found one pearl of great worth, went and sold all that he had, and bought it.' Cheyenne I'm trying to buy it."

She gasped, pushed him away, and said, "I knew it! It was you all the time."

"What are you talking about?" Harrison asked.

Cheyenne drew him closer and leaned her head against his chest. She didn't want this dance to ever end.

When the song ended, Harrison asked, "Would you like to go get a drink and sit down for a minute?"

"That would be nice," she said politely. She couldn't remember intentionally trying to be polite to him before.

They were quiet. Finally, Harrison said, "Cheyenne, we didn't get off on the right foot. I want to apologize for being a jerk. Everything you ever said about me was true and I deserved the award you gave me."

"What award was that?" she asked. She couldn't remember any award, but she couldn't remember much of anything at the moment.

"The 'legend-in-my-own-mind' award," he answered. "But now I would like to try again. Let's say, a fresh start. How about if I pick you up tomorrow night, Christmas Eve? You can ride with me to help deliver the presents to our family. And 'no' is not an acceptable answer."

"GQ, I mean Harrison, I would love to go with you. What time?"

"What's this GQ stuff, anyway?" he asked.

"Oh, nothing. Well, if you have to know, it's your nickname."

"A term of endearment, huh?"

"Yeah, something like that."

"You're not even going to argue with me? I was prepared to do some serious dealing, negotiating, whatever it took to get you to go with me," said Harrison.

"Go where?" she asked.

"Cheyenne, are you with me? I just asked you, no I told you, I was picking you up tomorrow night to go deliver the presents. I remind you that you already said, 'Yes,' so you can't change your mind now."

"Darn," she said. "I knew I should have held out. I could have gotten a meal out of the deal too." Then she laughed and tightened her grip on his hand.

Just then Jake walked over.

"Nice timing, Jake," Cheyenne said.

"What did you say, Cheyenne?" he asked.

"Nothing. It's just that you always seem to be around every time I want you to come by and rescue me," she winked.

"What are you talking about, Cheyenne?" Jake asked.

"Hey, she's not making a lot of sense to me either," Harrison said.

Jake decided he would get a more coherent response from Harrison. "Harrison, would you mind if I borrow Cheyenne for a few moments?" he asked.

"Not now, Jake," Cheyenne replied. "Can't it wait for a minute?"

Harrison could tell it couldn't wait, so he released her and said, "Sure, Jake. I have some things to take care of anyway. I'll see you tomorrow night, Cheyenne." With that, he left.

Jake looked at Cheyenne and asked, "Are you okay?"

She nodded. "I was until you came along."

"Walk with me next door for a moment, will you?" he asked.

"I may as well, seeing as you just ruined a perfect moment." Cheyenne smiled. She was feeling wonderful, like a kid on Christmas morning who had received every gift she wanted and more.

"Are you sure you're okay, Cheyenne? You're acting a little strange."

"Am not!" she exclaimed.

"Cheyenne, I'm just not sure where to begin. But you know that Nichole and I are very close, right?"

"Yes, she thinks you are the greatest."

"Well, it's a little complicated to explain, but it's something like this. Nichole kind of asked me to tell you some things, without really asking me to tell you. Do you understand?"

"Yeah, sure, Jake. It's clear as mud."

"It's still too hard for Nichole to talk about. I think it's like she wants you to know, but she doesn't want you to know that she knows you know."

"You really know how to make things simple, don't you?"

"All I can say is it must be one of those female things. So it's like this. She wants you to know but not to tell anyone you do. Now, do you understand what I am trying to tell you?"

Cheyenne looked at him, blinked, and said, "Would you say that one more time? Things have been a little fuzzy around here lately. Maybe you should try it in Tongan."

"Well, there is just one way to say this, so I should stop beating around the bush," Jake laughed. "Okay, it's like this. You asked me once why Nichole and Richard didn't have any kids, and I told you that it was a story for another day. Well, Nichole did have a child—a little girl, but she died after living for only three months. The child, had she lived, would have been about your age. Her death broke Nichole's heart. The necklace she gave you, the pendant with the mended heart, was her symbol of that love. Nichole felt she would always have a broken heart."

"Oh, no wonder! I'm so sorry. That explains so much. Nichole is the nicest person in the whole world. I can only imagine how she must have felt all of these years."

"She never forgot," Jake continued. "That's why she wore the necklace. One day, she was thinking about her daughter when she had a feeling; she knew there was a child out there who needed a mother. She knew it!

"She started her search and she would not be deterred. She told everyone she would know who the child was when she found her. She said she would just know. It wasn't long before one of the social workers told her about you. From that moment on, she knew you were the one. It didn't matter what the social worker, the judge, or anyone said. She knew you needed a mother as much as she needed a daughter. The Spirit touched her as she read about you and learned about your life. She knew she should adopt you—she felt it in her heart. You are her miracle, and she . . . well, I guess she is a mother again, the mother she always wanted to be."

Cheyenne was overwhelmed with emotion and could barely speak. "Jake, you will never know how much I love Nichole. I told her the other night that she was the mother I never had. I even called her Mom, and I think she liked it. It made me feel so good. Do you have any idea what it's like for me to have someone I can call Mom? Well, I've waited seventeen years to be able to call someone that, and it was worth every single minute of the wait."

Jake had a hard time talking, "Cheyenne, now you know why I am so proud of you. You mended the broken heart of one of the dearest people I have ever known. For that I will always be grateful."

"No, Jake, I didn't mend her broken heart. Love did. Love was her gift to me, like the gift Christ gave to us," Cheyenne said. "I was the lucky one."

Chapter 11

DECEMBER 23

Cheyenne couldn't remember touching the ground that day on the way home; somehow she found herself on her street. She had a family! *Have I really filled a hole in Nichole's life?* she wondered. Coming home felt wonderful, and she knew Nichole would be there, waiting to meet her and to listen to every detail of her day. All Cheyenne wanted was to be able to share her joy with Nichole.

In the telling, she knew she would experience those feelings all over again. She wasn't sure if she could exactly describe her emotions, but she knew they were intense—almost overpowering, and somewhere between rapture, unbelief, pain, thrill, and panic. Maybe Nichole could help her understand them. She wanted Nichole to know and feel what she had felt, but Cheyenne knew she would love telling her about Harrison no matter what the outcome. Nichole always made it that way.

Cheyenne was presented with an array of Christmas scents when she opened the door—the smell of newly cut evergreen and freshly baked bread caught her attention. Cookies were spread across the counter, and in the middle was a three-year-old fruitcake. Nichole was wearing jeans and a sweater, both of which showed evidence of a day spent in the kitchen. It was a scene Cheyenne wanted to remember. Nichole looked like a mom, but she was cuter, much cuter.

Cheyenne threw her books on a chair and walked into the kitchen. She pulled a gob of cookie dough out of the bowl and plopped it into her mouth.

"Hey, you'll ruin your dinner, missy," Nichole scolded.

"So how was your day?" Cheyenne asked. She sat on a bar stool and looked at Nichole. As much as she wanted to blurt it out, to tell her all about her day, Cheyenne wanted to know about Nichole's day. She wanted to know about Nichole's dreams, her feelings, and her life. So she said, "No, before I tell, and there's a lot to tell, I want to know about you and your day. I want to know how you feel."

"My day? You're kidding! Oh well, you know—drive the kids to school, basketball, piano lessons, dance class, and then hit the store in between. You know, the same ol', same ol'. Now quit stalling and tell me!"

"All right! But before I do, you have to promise to tell me about you. All we talk about is me, and I want to know about you, Mom."

"I promise, I promise! But not today. I have been dying to hear what happened at school," Nichole said.

"It was all too amazing," Cheyenne replied. "I'm afraid if I pinch myself, I am going to wake up and find myself back at the detention home missing one glass slipper. I can't believe all of this is happening to me."

"So you found out who was spending the big bucks on the white roses?"

"I can't tell you that now—it would be out of order. I have to start at the beginning. Do you want to ruin the whole story? I'll bet you are probably one of those people who read the last page of a book before anything else."

"How did you know?" Nichole asked.

Excited, she looked at Cheyenne and waited for her to begin.

Nichole was like a kid sometimes—eager and impatient, with eyes that sparkled like firelight. Her enthusiasm was contagious. She couldn't just sit there; she had to say something, and it just came bubbling out. "Cheyenne, you look lovely, I'm so excited for you. Now tell me everything, and tell me he kissed you."

"Mother!"

They laughed and Nichole listened intently to Cheyenne's story of her wonderful day. The only problem was that Nichole kept interrupting, asking for more detail. When Cheyenne finished, Nichole hugged her. Cheyenne felt good. She felt so alive. She tried to lighten the situation and said, "Tell me I don't have flour handprints on the back of my new dress."

"A little flour never hurt anything. It will wash right out," Nichole replied.

Cheyenne turned her head to wipe her cheeks. Nichole said, "Not you too."

"It seems like that's all I do lately," Cheyenne said, hugging Nichole even harder.

Cheyenne reached into her purse after Nichole released her. She extracted a small package wrapped in shiny silver paper and handed it to Nichole. "I want you to have this, Mom."

Tears of joy ran down Nichole's face. She tried to wipe them away so she could see, but more just kept coming. "I'm having a problem," she said. "For some reason, I can't see."

"It would help if you would quit crying, Mom," Cheyenne said as she wiped her own cheeks.

Finally, Nichole shrugged and said, "I guess it's a girl thing." She took the package and carefully unwrapped it. Inside the box was a beautiful silver heart pendant on a silver rope. The heart was flawless. Nichole picked up the necklace and fastened it around her neck. She hugged Cheyenne again and said, "This will always remind me of you, Cheyenne."

"There's a note in the box, Mom."

Nichole looked in the box, wiped her eyes, and removed the white linen card. She opened it and read aloud.

That which was lost is found
That which was broken has healed
Love forever, your daughter, Cheyenne

Nichole suddenly realized that she no longer carried the pain of her daughter's death. It seemed that no matter what she had done for the past sixteen years, she still carried that burden. She never let it show, but it had always been there. She carefully prodded the memories and discovered nothing but peace. She looked at Cheyenne and knew the reason. She also knew that Cheyenne knew.

"I guess Jake told you, right?" Nichole asked.

Cheyenne nodded.

"I lost my only child when she was three months old," Nicole explained. "It broke my heart. I lived for seventeen years with that pain, wondering what I had done wrong. Then one day, I started listening instead of asking, 'Why me?' I quit feeling sorry for myself. It was then that the Lord led me to you, Cheyenne. You know, what's really funny is that all this time you thought I was rescuing you when it was really you who held the magic. It was you who healed my heart when you first called me Mom, the words I never thought I would hear in this life. What I hope is that I can be as good a mom to you as you are a daughter to me."

Cheyenne again wondered what she had done to deserve a mother like Nichole. Cheyenne put her arms around her and held her. Then she said, "Do you mean I waited and suffered all these years for you to find me, just because you weren't listening?"

They were both having trouble speaking because of their joy. Finally Cheyenne said, "Hey, you said you were going to teach me how to make dinner rolls tonight, unlike last time when you started a flour fight."

"Me? It wasn't me who started that flour fight," replied Nichole with a mischievous grin.

"Go change out of your dress. I wouldn't want it to get ruined. Besides, you may end up looking like me. That is if you really get into it."

"That good, huh?" Cheyenne replied.

"Only if you're lucky," Nichole said.

The conversation came easily while they worked in the kitchen. "So if I understand it correctly," Nichole said, "you thought it was Harrison all along, and he finally admitted it to you while you were dancing."

"He didn't actually admit it, not at first. But then he asked me why I thought he would do something like that. Then he said he was looking to buy a pearl of great worth; at least that is what I thought he said. Things were a little fuzzy by then. And I even forgot to follow up on the question and make him admit it was him."

"So you don't know for sure?"

"Yeah, I know—at least I think I know. But now that you ask, I'm not sure I do."

"Okay, so if he is passionately in love with you, how come he played like the invisible man for the past two weeks?"

"Mom! I didn't say he was passionately in love with me. He tried to deflect the blame. He said it was my fault he hadn't said much the past two weeks. Funny, I can't remember much of what he said when we were dancing. He said something about the kids at the hospital, but I really can't remember what it was." After a pause, she asked, "When you were dating Richard, were there times when you had trouble thinking or forming long sentences, like sentences with two or more words?"

"I had trouble breathing," Nichole replied.

Suddenly Cheyenne remembered something and interrupted Nichole in midsentence. "I'm sorry, but I just remembered. Did you get the letter from Jake's grandfather yet?"

"Didn't I tell you I got it last week? I'm sure I told you, but you have been kind of spacey lately.

"Let me tell you about the letter," said Nichole. "Getting that letter was no easy task. First, I had to explain to Jake's father what I wanted and why. I wasn't sure he understood. His English is very broken. Then he had to call a relative on the island who talked to a friend who knew Jake's grandfather. This friend then talked to Jake's grandfather, and heaven only knows if he understood why we wanted the letter. His grandfather, of course, wrote the letter in Tongan. When I got it, I told his father that I couldn't read Tongan. So I sat down with Jake's father, and we translated the letter into broken English. I had his father read the translation and, you know, even though the language is broken, it sounds better read that way. More realistic. I think you are going to love the letter. And Jake, wow! By the way, and not to change the subject, did the class decide what they were going to give Jake?"

"Can't tell; it's a secret. You will get to see if you are at the seminary building for the meeting after we deliver the presents to our family. We are going to give it to him right after we get back to the seminary building. If you want, you can have his father read the letter."

Cheyenne knew it would be difficult to get Jake's father to the seminary building that late at night, so she said, "We could have Richard read the letter if you want."

Nichole laughed and said, "Richard can't read—not with feeling, not in an emotional setting. It would sound like he was reading a parts list out of the *AutoTrader*. No, I asked Jake's father to come and do the reading. He will be great."

"I think that will be perfect," Cheyenne replied. "You had better bring him or he won't get there on time." Nichole told Cheyenne not to worry about the details; she would handle them. "All you have to worry about is Harrison."

They finished their third batch of cookies and retrieved three loaves of bread from the oven. The smell was intoxicating, and the bread tasted even better than it smelled.

Cheyenne sat on a bar stool, savoring her third slice of bread. "Tell me about Christmas Eve and Christmas Day at the Lloyd home, at our home. I've often wondered how real families celebrate Christmas."

Nichole sat down beside her, thought for a minute, and said, "You've seen that sign that hangs in our entry all year long, right?"

"You mean the one that says, 'I believe in Santa Claus'?" Cheyenne asked.

"The very one," Nichole confirmed. "Well, you see, Richard told me the first Christmas we were together that if I didn't believe, Santa would pass me by. And he meant it. Around here, everyone gets spoiled on Christmas. Santa doesn't hold back if you believe. And wait until you see the socks we hang by the chimney. You could put two men and a dog in each of them. Come Christmas morning, they will be filled. The socks are always my favorite. Let me show them to you."

She went over to a box lying on the floor by the fireplace. She pulled from the box one of the biggest socks Cheyenne had ever seen. It was made of green felt with white Christmas decorations. It measured maybe four and a half feet from top to bottom and was about as round as Cheyenne's waist. Written in white felt down the sock was the name "Nichole."

Cheyenne responded, "Now that's a sock! How in the world can you ever fill one of those?"

Nichole didn't answer her question but pulled out two more socks about the same size. The first one was red and was labeled "Richard," and the third one was newer than the other two. It was white with red letters spelling out the name "Cheyenne." Cheyenne took the sox and held it up. "I can't wait for Christmas," she whispered.

Nichole sat down on the couch and said, "Thursday you and I will have to do our last-minute shopping, have lunch, and then find something very *chocolatey*. The celebration starts Thursday night on Christmas Eve. We usually go to my sister's house around six for dinner. It's wild—kids running everywhere. They are so excited they can't sit still. Then the 'real' Santa shows up with a bag of gifts, one for each of the kids, which most likely, will include you this year, Cheyenne."

"You mean me? I'm not a kid!"

"Well, don't tell Rich . . . I mean Santa. He might take you seriously, and you don't want to miss out. Besides, he wouldn't listen to you anyway."

Nichole continued, "Be careful because you will have to go sit on Santa's knee and talk to him in order to get the present. And be advised that our Santa tends to flirt with the cute girls.

"After that, we try to settle all the urchins down—not an easy task on Christmas Eve. Then we have our own little family performance of the birth of our Savior. You might be scheduled to play the part of Mary this year, so don't faint when they tell you. After the pageant, we all head our separate ways. In a way, that part of the night has always been a little sad for Richard and me because when we head out, it is just us; and you know what they say, Christmas is for kids. At least that's what I thought until I met Richard. He makes me feel like a kid again. He makes me crazy. First, I can't go to sleep. Then I wake up five times during the night and stare at the clock. Finally, I can't take it any longer, and I put both feet in his back and push. He always fakes like he is asleep and asks if he can just sleep for fifteen more minutes. But I know he is as eager as I am to see what the Jolly Ol' Fat Man left for me under the tree. Christmas is exciting for me because of Richard."

"He really loves you, doesn't he?" Cheyenne asked.

"He makes it all worth it," Nichole responded. "Cheyenne, I think one of the reasons Richard goes to such extremes at Christmas is because he didn't want me to feel left out because we didn't have any children. But we don't have that problem any more. I have a feeling you are going to be one spoiled kid, I mean young lady, come Christmas morning. He told me just the other day that Christmas is for kids as he was hiding more presents in the guest room. I tried to get in to see what he had stuffed in there, but he has all the keys and he won't let me see. I tried bribery, but it didn't work either. I even said I would be nice."

"But I don't have much of anything to give to you and Richard."

"Cheyenne, your gift to us can't be purchased in any store. I can't tell you how much having you around our house has meant to me. No, Cheyenne, if I didn't get anything for Christmas except you calling me mom, I would still feel like I was the richest person in the whole world. I have waited a long time for someone to call me Mom. But don't worry about me going without; Richard won't let that happen."

That night, before Cheyenne climbed into bed, she knew she had to do some serious explaining and thanking. She dropped to her knees and began to pray like she had never prayed before. She wanted to talk to her Father in Heaven. She was going to pray just like Jake told her to. "Talk to him like he was sitting in the chair next to you," he had said. "That's how prayers should be—personal." Cheyenne was on her knees for some time before she started to speak. First, she thanked her Father for her old life—the time before the Lloyds. She knew she had learned a lot about life during that time, even though it had been so hard. Then she thanked him more for giving her the Lloyds. She explained to him how much everything mattered now; how much peace she felt learning of her Father in Heaven. She told him all of the things in her heart. Last, she promised him that she would try to be the best person she could be, not for herself and not just for him, but for Nichole, Richard, Jake, and everyone. She wanted to make him proud of her.

She didn't hear any words, and she didn't see a vision, but she did feel at peace with herself and her God, and that mattered more than she ever imagined it could.

On Thursday morning, Cheyenne got up early, before Nichole and Richard, and made breakfast. She was not the best cook, but she could handle scrambled eggs, bacon, and Belgian waffles. She was quite proud of her efforts. Cheyenne wore an apron and had just finished the final touches when Richard came into the kitchen. "Wow! Maybe you could teach Nichole . . ." just as Nichole punched him in the arm and said, "Teach me what, Buster?"

"Nothing, nothing."

They all sat down and, after a short prayer, had breakfast.

Nichole finished and said, "We can get a jump on the crowd if we leave now. Let's go, Cheyenne. Richard can do the dishes."

"What?" he exclaimed. "But—"

"But nothing. We have some girl things to do. See you in a while and don't forget to start the dishwasher," Nichole instructed. Cheyenne shrugged and smiled at Richard.

"I know! Girl things in her language means shopping," Richard said. "Have fun and think of me back here slaving away in the kitchen."

As they drove to the mall, Cheyenne confessed some of her feelings and misgivings to Nichole. "I'm nervous about going with Harrison tonight."

"Oh, it's Harrison now, not the GQ guy?" Nichole teased with a sly grin on her face.

"Well, that depends on how I am feeling at the moment. Right now, I can't seem to focus. I can't even remember what clothes he was wearing. All I can remember is the smell of his cologne and his eyes—the name GQ doesn't do justice to his eyes."

"So tell me why you're nervous," Nichole said.

"I don't know how to act around someone like him. I don't even know what to talk about. I'm afraid I will say something stupid; or worse, not be able to respond to questions with answers reflecting intelligence above a third-grade level. I'm afraid I won't look good. I'm just intimidated, plain and simple. What do I do? What do I say?"

"Remember, if you ever say or do something really stupid, you always have an excuse—just use it. Say, 'It's okay, you can't hold that against me because I'm just having a blonde day,' and go on like nothing unusual or out of the ordinary happened."

Cheyenne laughed. "Are you serious?"

"Dead serious. And say it like you mean it. Besides, it's cute.

"Second," she continued, "I really don't think you are going to have to worry about stupid comments. He is so starstruck that he won't know the difference. You know that a good-looking blonde makes men helpless," Nichole said.

"And last, always think offense. Besides, Cheyenne, he is

one lucky guy to be able to take you. Just because he has a little money doesn't cut it with me. Now the fact that he is a adorable . . . well, that matters, so we will be a little nicer to him."

"I like your spunk," Cheyenne responded, "but it's easier said than done. I've been there and I don't think very well on my feet, particularly when he makes contact with me like he did when we were dancing. Even two-syllable words are challenging."

"Cheyenne, this is the time of your life for making memories. You will always look back on these days. The newness, the firsts, love—it's all rolled into one ball, and it has its own momentum once it gets rolling. It's hard to stop or even to slow down. It's the most exciting time of life. Cheyenne, don't be afraid of it. Learn to take it on your terms. You never have to compromise who you are or what you believe. If someone tries to tell you otherwise, then get rid of him, and that includes Mr. GQ. Remember, you are someone special and deserve to be treated that way. If someone messes up, then he is going to have to deal with me."

"Nichole, I'm so excited to go with Harrison tonight, but that's only half of it. Can you imagine what our little family is going to say when they see the big box sitting on the steps of their trailer with presents spilling out everywhere? I hope Jane understands and loves my good-luck necklace as much as I did."

Nichole looked at Cheyenne. "I have heard from parents, teachers, and others the story of the big box and of Jake. Of course, everyone loves to tell their own version of the story. Seems Jake has become a legend among the parents, and the administration at Granite thinks he is the greatest. He is a great example, not only for Polynesian students but also for everyone. He has set the standard and shown them they can make it if they are willing to reach upward. I am so happy for him. I think his grandfather was right. I think he knew Jake would be a leader. Jake is some kind of guy."

Nichole had some gifts to buy and two items to pick up that were on hold. As they passed the shoe store, she said, "Cheyenne, I know you are short of funds and I know Richard would love those shoes. What if I buy them and you give them to him?"

"That wouldn't be right. Why don't you just give them to him?" Cheyenne inquired.

Nichole paid for the shoes and handed them to Cheyenne. "You have to wrap them and make sure they are labeled from you. Now it's time to find some chocolate."

When they got home, Nichole told Cheyenne to go wrap all of her presents and get everything ready to put under the tree. "When you have finished, come into the downstairs game room. That's where I have Richard's stuff. You will have to help me get his things wrapped and ready to put under the tree before you leave with Harrison, okay?"

The Christmas spirit was contagious. Nichole made it fun. By five, Cheyenne was dressed and ready to spend her first real Christmas Eve with her family. Dinner at Nichole's sister's house was fun and hectic all at the same time. Cheyenne was treated like a celebrity by all of the family members. Then Santa came. She noticed that Santa's shoes looked awfully familiar. It wasn't long before Santa called out, "Cheyenne, come on up here, darlin'. I think there's a present in this bag for you. Santa always remembers the good-lookin' girls."

Cheyenne was embarrassed, but she walked up to Santa amid the cheers and hollers of the entire family. She stood next to him and he reached up and pulled her down to sit on his knee. Between belly laughs, he said, "What does a good-looking young lady like you want from Santa? By the way, you're not on my naughty list this year, are you?"

Cheyenne replied, "You mean that's why I never got anything for Christmas, because I made your bad list? Well, I think I just got permanently off that list. At least that's what my Christmas elf told me this morning. If that's the case, then I want you to bring me—I can't tell you because it's a wish and if I say, it won't happen."

Santa laughed. "Dearie, you might just get your wish. Santa

has his ways, you know. You look around your Christmas tree in the morning. But I think I have a present for you tonight. Yes, here it is." He handed it to her and she tried to stand up. He laughed, "No, you don't get to leave until you've opened it and given old Santa a hug. Santa doesn't get to hug many young beautiful girls any more. At least since he got married, that is."

Cheyenne ripped open the package as fast as she could. It was a recent photo of Richard and Nichole, arms around each other, in front of their Christmas tree. It was signed, "Mom and Dad, Christmas Eve." Cheyenne stood up, pulled Santa to his feet, and threw her arms around him. She kissed him on the cheek. "Thanks, Santa."

"And I heard Christmas was just for kids!" Santa said.

Cheyenne stepped back but Santa held her arm, pulled her back into an embrace, and said, "You don't get away from Santa that easy. I get one more hug for the road. Now don't you go and tell Mrs. Santa about these hugs, okay?"

By that time everyone was laughing and shouting. Cheyenne was right in the middle of one big, happy family.

When they got home that night, Richard holed up in "his" room and told them that no one could come in, and no excuses. Cheyenne helped Nichole finish her wrapping, and they put the presents around the tree. Next, they took the stockings out and placed each one on the back of a chair that had been so designated. Cheyenne kept watching the clock, wondering why time was going so slow.

Nichole laughed and asked, "Don't you think you should go get ready? I think Harrison will be here any minute."

Cheyenne was both excited and nervous at the same time. Finally, there was a soft knock at the door. Cheyenne glanced into the mirror one more time and tried to straighten her hair. She took a deep breath and opened the door. Harrison stepped inside looking better than ever.

As she introduced Harrison to her family, she said, "Mom and Dad, I would like you to meet Mr. GQ—I mean, Harrison Daniels. He only looks like he stepped out of the pages of

Gentleman's Quarterly. He shook hands with Richard and Nichole. Then he handed Cheyenne a white rose in a crystal vase.

"This is for you."

Cheyenne took the vase, glanced at Nichole and then back at Harrison. "I knew it was you all along," she said.

"Anyone who goes to such lengths to get a girl's attention gets my vote," Nichole chimed in.

"No, you didn't know it was me. You might have suspected, but you didn't know for sure," Harrison replied.

Cheyenne shocked herself because she suddenly put her arms around Harrison and hugged him. "I guess I hoped it was you. But if it wasn't you, then I guess I'll have to find the mystery man and hug him too."

"Okay, it was me. I promise," admitted Harrison. "You don't need to start looking for other guys to shower with your affection. I am the guilty party."

"Sorry, we have to run," Harrison said to everyone. "If we don't, we will miss the big show." He turned to face Cheyenne and said, "That coat is not going to be warm enough. It is really snowing out there tonight." Cheyenne retrieved her parka and they headed for the door.

"Have fun! We'll see you later tonight at the seminary building," Nichole said enthusiastically.

Harrison closed the door, took Cheyenne's hand, and led her out to his car. Cheyenne stopped and looked. She didn't see a brand-new Beamer; she saw a used Ford pickup truck. Cheyenne slid into the seat when Harrison opened the door for her. Cheyenne waited until he climbed in, and then she slid over to sit close to him. "Is this your second car?" Cheyenne asked as they drove off.

"Well, no, this is the only car I have now," replied Harrison.

"Let me guess, you had a fight with your father and he took the Beamer away."

"You mean you only wanted to go out with me because of the Beamer?" he replied.

Cheyenne knew he was trying to avoid her question, but she

was not going to let him off that easily. "Out with it," she encouraged him. "Tell me what happened to your car."

"No, it's just that I didn't really want to tell anyone."

Cheyenne knew she had hit a soft spot and decided not to push it. "Okay, you're off the hook. You don't have to tell me if you don't want to."

"You don't understand, Cheyenne. Let me try to explain. You see, I have never before sacrificed anything—never in my life. I didn't understand until I saw you give your necklace, your most precious possession, to our family. It was then that I decided to sell the Beamer. With the proceeds, I got this Ford and still had enough money to buy all the presents I gave to our family. But I don't want anyone to know. I had to do this for me. Do you understand?"

Cheyenne looked again at Harrison. She knew she had misjudged him, and she was suddenly proud of him. Finally, she said, teasing, "Well, I guess you'll have to take me back home if you don't have the Beamer. I mean, what will everyone think?"

Harrison looked at her like he had been slapped in the face. Cheyenne couldn't hold it in any longer, and she started to laugh. She squeezed his arm and said, "Maybe you are a keeper after all."

Jake got to the seminary building about 11:15 P.M., which was early, and he never got anywhere early. He was nervous and started pacing about the room. There wasn't a soul anywhere. The parking lot was empty except for two feet of snow on the ground. It was going to be a white Christmas. It had started snowing at about 10 P.M. and had snowed steadily since. Jake said out loud, "No way those kids will get here tonight, not in this weather. They would be crazy. So how in the world am I going to get all these presents over to our family by myself?"

Despite his worries, he opened the building and turned on the lights and heater. Then he went into his classroom to wait and see what would happen. It got to be 11:30 and still no one was there. Jake began to pace. He looked out the window one more time and saw a stream of headlights pulling into the parking lot, and he said a quick prayer of thanks.

Cheyenne and Harrison were in one of the first cars that pulled into the parking lot. Cheyenne stepped out of the car into the freshly fallen snow. Cheyenne grabbed Harrison's arm and wouldn't let go, not tonight. He helped her take off her coat as they entered the classroom. Jake looked at them and said, "Glad you could make it. I wasn't sure anyone would show up."

Soon the room was full. But it wasn't just Jake's students, it was other kids from school who had joined the project without being asked. And there were some parents and even some brothers and sisters. Everybody who had been involved in filling the big box was there.

The room was full of would-be Santas, excited to share the Christmas spirit with their little family. They were bursting at the seams with happiness and excitement, and each knew this would be a Christmas they would never forget. They had discovered the joy of Christmas and the essence of gift giving, and Cheyenne could see that Jake was proud.

Cheyenne had never seen so many excited smiles. She knew it was because they had all given to the family, never thinking of themselves. *This is going to be so great,* Cheyenne thought.

Everyone wanted to know how they were going to pull off the surprise delivery of so many packages, and everyone seemed to ask at the same time, "Jake, how're we gonna do this?" Jake had gathered several parents together to coordinate the effort. All of a sudden, the seminary door crashed open and the crowd went silent.

All eyes were on Mitch, a hulk who strode into the room. Mitch played football until he got kicked off the team for disciplinary problems. In fact, Jake had tossed him out of his seminary class earlier in the year because he was so disruptive. He was loud, obnoxious, and would rather fight than talk. He was just plain mean but someone you'd want on your side in a fight.

150

He didn't say a word as he walked right up to Jake's desk. He was carrying a box that was so big it would have taken two regular students to carry. He set it on the desk in front of Jake with a loud thump and dusted the snow off of the top. The room was still silent with all eyes on Mitch. No one knew what to expect.

Mitch looked Jake straight in the eye and loudly said, "Open it up."

Jake was speechless but finally responded, "I'm sorry, what was that? What did you say?"

Mitch repeated himself. "Open it up."

Jake replied, "Are you sure?"

Mitch was getting a little impatient. "Yeah, just open the box."

So not knowing what to expect, Jake opened the box. It was filled with things wrapped in white butcher paper. They were labeled: hamburger, T-bone steak, rump roast, and other prime beef.

Jake smiled, looked up at Mitch, and asked, "Where did you get this?"

Mitch broke into a huge smile. "Well, my dad's a butcher and he is drunk most of the time. When I saw him tonight, he was at it again. He wasn't feelin' anything. So I sneaked in and took all of this beef out of the freezer. He'll never even notice it's gone."

"Why did you do that?" Jake asked.

Mitch kicked the floor, trying to divert all the attention and said, "Well, I heard about your little deal here, and I thought your family could use some meat."

He looked at Jake with clouded eyes. "Can I come along with you guys tonight and help make the delivery?"

Suddenly Craig yelled, "Good show, Mitch," and everyone else chimed in, "Way to go, Mitch."

Mitch ran with the wild crowd and was always in trouble. He was junkyard mean. Yet he had been touched by the Spirit, and now he wanted more. Jake kept smiling and slapped Mitch on the back.

"You sure can! That is, if you will carry this box of meat out to the truck. I don't know if I can lift it."

Jake quieted everyone down. "This is what we're going to do," he began. He drew a map on the chalkboard so everyone would know where they were going.

"Now, here is where we are going to park," he said, marking an X on the map. "It's less than a block from the trailer on a little hill. From this point, you will all be able to see what happens when our family discovers the presents."

He added, "Now you guys who are driving the trucks with all of the presents, I want you to drive right here," and he made another X on the map. "That is as close as we can get to the trailer. Actually, it's in front of a lot next door to the trailer."

Harrison was standing in the back of the room holding Cheyenne's hand. He was excited and joined in every chorus of shouts. Cheyenne was glowing with happiness but remained quiet and didn't want to break the spell. Her heart was racing, but she was breathing a little easier.

"Now, the most important thing I am going to tell you," Jake continued, "is that there is a gag order in place from the minute you get out of your cars. I don't want anyone talking. Any noise and we will be discovered. After the sleighs—I mean pickups—get in position, we will all walk down to them, form a human chain, and pass the presents from one person to the next. The last person will stack them on the porch. But we have to be very quiet. Does everyone understand?"

"Whatever you say, Jake," they all said.

Jake went on. "Okay, everyone start hauling the presents out to the trucks, but be careful not to drop anything." Mitch had borrowed his father's meat van, and before long it was loaded with packages. Craig had brought his souped-up Ford pickup just in case they needed extra space. In fact, a few of the last-minute gifts were placed in the back of his truck. A tarp was thrown over the bed to keep the snow off of the presents until they got to their destination and, of course, Craig directed the loading of his truck. He didn't want any scratches on his beauty.

Mitch jumped into the car and donned his Santa hat. He sang

out, "On Dasher, on Donner . . . " but his voice was drowned out by the engine of the van. Jake filled his car with students, and off they went.

The snow continued to fall, and except for the noise of the engines, the night was calm and quiet.

Chapter 12

1 A.M.
DECEMBER 25

Jake pulled over and everyone climbed out. The rest of the cars found places close by, and the pickups pulled ahead and stopped down the hill closer to the trailer. Harrison opened the door for Cheyenne, who stepped out into the magical Christmas Eve night. The secret Santas quietly crowded around, and with bridled enthusiasm checked out the lay of the land. They all saw the little trailer.

Cheyenne could almost hear the silence of the falling snow. Dancing snowflakes reminded her of miniature Christmas ornaments floating through the air. The pristine snow was getting deeper. Streetlights were muted golden by the falling snow, and houses were warmly snuggled away for the night under a fresh, white blanket.

There was something else: a spirit, a Christmas spirit that seemed to burst on the scene as if carried by those swirling flakes. The group stood spellbound, staring into the night toward the little trailer that was buried in snow. It looked dark, forlorn, like something lost or forgotten, something Santa might even miss on this magical Christmas night.

But Cheyenne knew otherwise. Her friends and classmates were so excited; it was if they were once again six years old, fully expecting to get a peek of the jolly old fat man and his eight reindeer as they glided down onto the top of that trailer. Their faces were aglow with intoxicating excitement and anticipation, yet they were amazingly quiet. They knew this night was not for them.

On the signal, everyone walked down the hill and formed a single file line. Some were wearing only windbreakers and gym shoes, but none felt the cold.

The brightly colored packages started flowing down the line. Cheyenne knew her necklace was there too. Each present represented sacrifice. These were not just plain, old, regular Christmas presents; these were special presents. They were packaged as though by the wise men for the baby in the manger, with all the love and hope of man.

The gifts were handled with care as they passed from hand to hand, never touching the snow. Cheyenne looked at her fellow students through misty eyes. She smiled because she knew they were making a difference. Cheyenne knew in her heart that tomorrow this little corner of the world would be just a little brighter, and in some small way, she had helped create some of that light.

"I have never been so proud," Jake whispered in a low, husky voice, quivering with emotion, to everyone and to no one in particular. "Oh, how I love you guys, every one of you." Cheyenne knew she would carry the memory of the magical night in her heart forever.

After the packages were placed on the porch, the pile was a sight to behold. Presents were stacked at least ten feet tall and entirely covered the porch. Jake motioned for everyone to follow him. He led them back out onto the street, where he gathered them together. "Here's what we're gonna do," he said.

Jake beckoned to Craig, a fast little running back. "Here's what I want you to do, Divet. I want you to jump this fence and sprint over to the porch, but be careful. When you get to the door of the trailer, I want you to hit it with your shoulder going full speed. Then I want you to get out of there as fast as you can. Do you understand me?"

Craig said, "No problem, man, it'll be a cakewalk."

Jake said, "No, I don't think you do understand, Divet. What I mean is, they have a dog."

Craig was unconcerned, "They have a dog? Well, why hasn't it awakened yet?"

Jake added, "It's hard of hearing and it sleeps right under a shed out back. I saw the dog just the other night."

Craig was fearless. "Well, I've been around a lot of dogs, but what kind of a dog did you say it was?"

"It's an old Lab. It stands well above my knee, and it's ornery and willing to fight anything. It tries to rip bumpers off cars. Now, I guarantee you, if you hit that door as hard as you can, this dog is going to wake up and come running after you."

"Okay, I got it," said Craig. He turned and ran toward the trailer as fast as he could go. He reached the porch and kept right on going, when all of a sudden his feet came out from under him. He landed on his back, slid up against the trailer, and made a whole lot of noise. Everyone held their breath and watched in horror. But he was up in a flash and back on his feet. Craig then hit the door with everything he had. Cheyenne thought he was going to knock it right off its hinges.

Then, just as quickly, Craig turned and was running back to where everyone stood. He ran as fast as he had ever run. The snow didn't seem to slow him a bit. He took the fence in a single leap and was soon standing in the middle of the group, panting heavily.

Everyone's attention was riveted on the trailer. Cheyenne stood in front of Harrison. He put his arms around her. He bent down and whispered in her ear, "Are you cold?"

"Not anymore," she said, leaning back into him.

Someone said, "What if they aren't home?"

Jake responded, "Then I guess we will have to sit out here until they get home. Anybody bring a heater?"

Chapter 13

EARLY CHRISTMAS MORNING

Jake herded everyone back to the top of the hill. Wild anticipation ran through the anxious group. Attention was focused on the little snowbound trailer as they waited for something to happen. No one climbed into a warm car. All were watching for some sign of life from the trailer.

Harrison leaned over and asked Cheyenne if she wanted to sit in the pickup for a minute to get warm, but no one could have gotten her into the pickup at such an exciting time. She didn't want to miss one second. Besides, Harrison was standing behind her with both arms wrapped around her, and she didn't feel any cold. Breathing, though, was beginning to be a problem—again. She couldn't have said anything even if she had wanted to. She was at a complete loss for words.

The group continued to watch, but no lights came on. No one moved. Two minutes passed. The night remained silent.

Cheyenne felt a spear of disappointment puncture her side. She so wanted to watch the family when they found the presents. She, along with everyone else, seemed to hold her breath, not knowing what to expect.

Finally, Jake spoke up and everyone seemed to exhale at the same time, "Divet, looks like you didn't hit that door hard enough. Are you ready for another go at it?"

At that instant, the door to the trailer opened just a crack.

Billy, a tiny five-year-old, poked his head through the door to see if he could figure out what had caused the noise. He was either dumbstruck or awed because he continued to turn his head to the right and left, obviously trying to comprehend what was stacked on his front porch. Without warning, he pushed the door open all the way, continuing to stare at the huge pile of presents. His arms were hanging limply at his sides. He didn't show any emotion whatsoever. He again looked back to the right and then to the left. He beheld the pile and appeared frozen in time. Then, all of a sudden, as if he figured it out, he began jumping up and down, hollering and screaming.

Cheyenne felt chills running up and down her back. As she looked at that little boy, she just knew that he was thinking, *Santa's sleigh crashed right here on my porch!*

As suddenly as he had started screaming and jumping, he stopped. He walked bare-footed over to the pile and stared for a full minute. Cheyenne didn't think anyone moved one step or even breathed. They watched as Billy got a huge smile on his face and started sifting through the packages. Finally, he stopped and picked up one of the packages, dusting the snow off. He read the name tag: "Billy." Then, like a flash, he ran back inside the trailer and slammed the door, taking the package with him.

Cheyenne looked around at her friends. Some were laughing, others were wiping their eyes. Jake had one arm on Craig's shoulder and the other on Mitch's shoulder. "Did you see the look on his face when he saw the pile?" Jake asked. A few people started chuckling. Everyone wanted to see what would happen next.

A hush fell on the group of well-doers as the door to the trailer slowly opened again. They could hear some muffled voices drifting across the snow and then some squeals and laughing. The words were loud and clear: "Mom, Dad, everyone, come and see!"

Harrison hugged Cheyenne even tighter. She knew he was feeling what she was feeling. Cheyenne didn't know which was more exciting—Harrison's arms around her or the goings-on at the trailer. She squeezed his arm and looked back to the trailer.

One light flashed on in a bedroom and another in the living room. Through the windows, shadows could be seen moving toward the front door. The whole family was soon standing in the doorway, staring in disbelief.

"See, I told you!" exclaimed Billy. The whole family was spellbound as they peered at the pile. Little Nate's head poked through his father's legs as he tried to see what all the commotion was about.

"I told you Santa wouldn't miss us this year," said Jane, the eleven-year-old. "There can't be this many presents in the whole world."

One by one, each of the family walked out onto the porch. They were still in shock, that is except for Billy, who had seen enough. He wanted another present with his name on it and was picking up one package after another. "This says 'Mom,' and this one's for you, Jane. Mom, there are lots with your name on them, too."

The family members were dressed in light pajamas, but they didn't seem to mind the chill. Fred, the father, held up his hand to shield his eyes. He looked around but didn't see anyone.

After a few seconds, Fred said to his family, "It's time to pray." They dropped to their knees right there in the doorway and bowed their heads. They listened as their father thanked God. When he had finished, Billy jumped up and ran to the edge of the porch. "If we look really hard, we might be able to see Santa and Rudolph and maybe his sleigh."

Billy sang out as loud as he could, "Thanks, Santa. I knew you would come. My dad didn't mean it. He knew you were coming all the time; he was just kidding us when he told us you wouldn't be coming this year."

Cheyenne had a huge lump in her throat, and all she wanted to do was cry. She looked as Jake watched over his charges. Jake was wiping his eyes, as were most of Cheyenne's friends.

Harrison whispered to Cheyenne, "I have never felt like this in my whole life. All I had to do was give." None of them talked or laughed; they just silently watched. Jake bowed his head and whispered a short prayer. He thanked God for each one of his students. After the prayer, Cheyenne reached over and squeezed his arm. "Jake," she said, "this is all because of you."

"Hey, guys," Fred said to his family, "let's get all this stuff inside before it gets wet." They formed a line and began passing the presents into the trailer.

Cheyenne saw Jane stop passing presents. "The paper on this one is beautiful and it's for me," Jane said. She pressed the little package to her chest. "Oh, thank you, Santa." Cheyenne knew it was her necklace. She stopped breathing and listened.

Waves of joy swept over Cheyenne. She watched Jane open the package, taking care not to tear the wrapping. She clasped the necklace to her chest. "Mom, this is the most beautiful necklace I have ever seen," Jane said solemnly. "Will you put it on for me?" Her mother walked over and helped her put on the necklace, and then she gave her a hug. "It looks lovely on you, Jane. But what's this note in the package?" Her mother read the note out loud.

> *Jane, this necklace is the most sacred possession I own. It is magic because it has the power to heal a broken heart. I hope it will come to mean as much to you as it means to me.*

The mother and father were crying and hugging each other and the children. The passing of presents had stopped, but now all of the children, all except for Jane, were eager to find more presents. Jane just stood there holding the necklace. Cheyenne was speechless, unable to breathe. Jake turned to her and said, "Now that's a gift well given and a gift well received."

Finally, all of the presents found their way into the trailer except for the box full of meat from Mitch. The father tried to pick it up, but it wouldn't budge. He said, "Dear, will you come help me with this?"

Both parents tried to pick it up, but it still just sat there. The father opened it and looked inside. He called to his kids and told them there was one last thing to carry in. "Get back in the line and let's stack them in the kitchen." One by one, packages of T-bone steaks, pot roast, and hamburger were carried into the house.

Big, tough Mitch was there next to Jake and reached over and punched him in the arm. Jake punched him back. The joy was contagious.

No one remembered to close the door, so the watchers could still see some of the goings-on. "Hey, you kids need to get to bed," the mother said. "We will open these presents in the morning."

Billy screamed as he tore the paper off of a package addressed to him and said, "Forget that! It's time for presents." Soon paper was flying through the air. The onlookers could see the silhouettes in the window. Kids were laughing and telling each other what they had just opened. The father drew his wife into his arms and they both just watched. "Hey, Mom, aren't you going to open yours?" came the excited young voice of Billy.

The watchers seemed to be barely breathing. The spirit was there and all were feeling it. No one wanted to leave, no one wanted to break the spell. Harrison continued to hold Cheyenne in his arms. Everything seemed frozen in time.

Jake bumped into Harrison, almost knocking both Cheyenne and Harrison over. "Excuse me. I didn't see you standing there," said Jake. "My, my, that isn't Cheyenne you've got your arms around, is it? Did Harrison tell you that Utah and Stanford have both offered him full-ride scholarships? And it isn't because he is good-looking."

Cheyenne gasped and hesitantly asked, "And so what did you tell them Mr. Hotshot quarterback? And is there a reason you haven't bothered to tell me about this little surprise, or was I going to find out after you left?"

Jake, the troublemaker, turned to talk to someone else. Cheyenne's heart sunk. Just when she let herself go. Just when she opened her heart, Mr. GQ, the object of her heart, was about to get out of Dodge. She knew it was too good to be true. She didn't belong in his world anyway.

She heard his voice. "Are you still with me, Cheyenne? Now let me try to answer your questions. One at a time, okay?" He looked sincere, like he wanted her to understand.

"You could at least have told me you were leaving the state before . . ." said Cheyenne, trailing off before she sank back into a silent trance. She thought, *It's okay, I'm only dating him. I'm not in love with him. I can do this.* But she wasn't convinced.

"Cheyenne, listen to me. I just found out. I haven't had time to tell you and besides, you wouldn't have listened or even cared before Wednesday. If you remember correctly, you could not even tolerate my presence. In fact, just last week didn't you ask me 'if it hurt?' And I responded, 'Hurt? What do you mean?' And you said, 'You know, when you fell from heaven.'"

The mood had been broken. Harrison wasn't even holding her hand. Cheyenne was sorry she had let Jake's comments upset her so much. After all, he was right. She decided she could at least be his friend. *Like that's really going to work,* she thought.

Cheyenne hesitantly responded, "I guess you would be crazy not to go to Stanford to play football. It's the opportunity of a lifetime. Is that what you decided, Harrison?" Suddenly that old feeling of loneliness seemed to swallow her up again.

In truth, Cheyenne felt crushed, totally deflated. She bowed her head, not wanting to hear the answer. All of a sudden, she felt herself being lifted from the ground and literally dropped in a huge snowdrift. She came up sputtering, trying to clear the snow off her face. She looked up to see two blue eyes with grey streaks peering down at her. They were full of mischief and only five inches away. "Now, what did you ask me?"

Suddenly she couldn't breathe again. *It must be the snow,* she thought, *or maybe the cold.* But she knew it wasn't the snow or the cold. In fact, she felt a little warm. She stammered, "Uh, what question?"

"Have you ever trusted anyone, Cheyenne?" Harrison asked.

163

Harrison bent lower and kissed her nose. He slowly stood up, took hold of both her arms, and lifted her back on her feet. She was covered in snow. Jake turned toward them. "Cheyenne, it's a little cold to be playing in the snow tonight, isn't it?"

Jake chuckled while Harrison dusted the snow off Cheyenne. When he had finished, he put his arms around her again.

Cheyenne giggled. Jake turned his attention back to them. "Will you quit acting like two teenage high school kids in love?"

He had said the words. *Is this what love feels like?* Cheyenne wondered.

Suddenly someone said something, and everyone's attention turned again to the trailer. Billy stuck his head out of the door and looked around one more time. He yelled as loudly as he could, "Thanks, Santa, wherever you are. We love you."

As everyone watched through the windows, planes were flying across the room, balls were tossed up and down, and clothes were held up to view.

Jake finally awoke everyone from their trance. "Okay, guys, let's all go back to the seminary building." One by one, the cars were started, turned around, and driven away from the snowy scene of a very merry Christmas. Cheyenne knew that something special had happened. It was a night she never wanted to end and always wanted to remember.

As they drove back to the seminary building, Cheyenne was surprised by the memories that came flooding through her mind. She stared out the window and listened to Johnny Mathis singing "I'll be Home for Christmas," and she knew that for the first time in her life, she had a "home" where she would be for Christmas.

"A penny for your thoughts?" Harrison asked.

"Oh, I was just thinking what a wonderful night this has been. I don't know if I've ever experienced the range of emotions I've felt tonight." She didn't want to tell him exactly what emotions she was talking about, so she asked him, "What about you, Mr. GQ?"

"Well, since you asked, I was thinking about the two things

that brought me here tonight—two things that turned me upside down and ran me through the ringer. I am a different person now. I hope I'm a better person.

"Remember when Jake asked me, no, forcefully took me, to Primary Children's Hospital to read to the kids."

"I didn't know that until yesterday," Cheyenne answered.

"Those kids are unbelievable," Harrison said as they pulled in front of the seminary building. "Jimmy, an eight-year-old with only one arm, makes me arm wrestle him every day, and he beats me every time. Then there's Sarah, a little four-year-old who has cancer. She asks me to hold her hand while we watch *Lady and the Tramp*. Each of those kids has stolen a piece of my heart. I was annoyed that Jake would make me go waste my time reading to kids. But then they got to me. Most of them will never walk out of that hospital, but they never think about their problems. They cared about me, the 'big football star.' They cared about their friend down the hall who was going to die. Cheyenne, I can't tell you how much those kids mean to me."

There was a long pause. It didn't feel right to break the silence. Eventually Cheyenne asked, "So what's the second thing?"

"Cheyenne, the second thing was you."

"Me?"

"I remember the first time I saw you and knocked you over going to football practice. Remember?"

"I remember only too well."

"Well, I remember the first time you came to class as a blonde. I remember you dancing with Robert, who is nice but nerdy. I remember Tom James walking you to class. I remember you teaching our class about giving when you had nothing to give. I remember wanting to talk to you and be with you. And you wouldn't give me the time of day."

"Would too! You just didn't ask."

"Every time I tried to talk to you, all you wanted to do was bite my head off."

"I didn't mean it. You should have figured that out."

"What?"

"The problem is that you just don't understand girls."

"No kiddin'!"

Then he spoke quietly. "Cheyenne, ever since that first day, there has only been one person I was interested in. It was you and I didn't know why. After you gave your speech to the class, I knew. There is no one else like you."

Cheyenne sat there staring at him. She wasn't sure she could say anything even if she could think of something to say. It was all too wonderful. She reached over and took his hand and drew it up to her lips, kissed the back of it, and then held it against her cheek. Finally she said, "I didn't think anyone like you could ever like someone like me."

"Cheyenne, I think you've got that backward. Money, clothes, and a car don't make a good person. You have the light. Everyone around you wants to share your light. You make everyone better. I just want to share in the light."

There was a knock at the window, and Jake motioned for Cheyenne to roll it down. "I don't want to break up anything, but you two should come into the building before the meeting is over."

"You have absolutely the worst timing of anybody I know," Cheyenne said to Jake.

It was still snowing. Harrison opened the door for Cheyenne and put his arm around her as they walked into the seminary building. Harrison pulled out two chairs, took her coat, and hung it to dry. Then he sat down and took her hand as they waited for everyone to settle down.

Nichole and Richard walked in holding hands. They looked great together. Cheyenne made them come over and sit by her and Harrison. Cheyenne saw Nichole look at their hands and she smiled. "Am I going to have to wait all night to hear what happened?"

Cheyenne said, "I promised Harrison that I wouldn't say a word."

Harrison leaned over toward Nichole and whispered, "She's not telling the truth. But if you want to know anything, I'll tell you." He winked and then said way too loudly, "She sure is cute, don't you think?"

Cheyenne blushed and tried to change the subject. She asked Nichole, "Did you get Mr. Wolfgramm?"

"Yes, but he's waiting outside until everyone gets here. We don't want Jake to see him yet."

Cheyenne decided to explain what had happened between Harrison and her. "Harrison pushed me, no, he lifted me up and threw me in a snowbank."

"You probably deserved it, Cheyenne," Richard responded. "Sometimes that's the only way to get a girl's attention. Isn't that right, Harrison?"

"Especially blondes," Harrison replied.

Cheyenne quietly told Nichole about Billy and how Jane had found her mended-heart necklace. Cheyenne then leaned over closely to Nichole and whispered something. Harrison could hear his name mentioned a couple of times, but he couldn't make out what she was saying. Nichole gave Cheyenne's hand a squeeze.

Meanwhile, everyone had assembled in the seminary room. The group was much more subdued. A quiet spirit of peace filled the room. Mitch walked in and sat up front. Craig was holding his shoulder and explaining to anyone who would listen how hard he had hit the door. Jake was just watching. Cheyenne knew he didn't want the night to end either.

Chapter 14

DECEMBER 25

A gentle calmness settled over the classroom. It was 2 A.M. Christmas Morning by the time the jubilant ragtag band had finally reconvened in the seminary classroom. Jake had been quiet but now stood up and said, "I have been listening to all of you share your experiences and your feelings. I am overwhelmed. I don't know what to say."

Craig fired back, "That's a first, Jake. You are never at a loss for words."

"You are right, Divet, but tonight has made me think back to a conversation I had a long time ago with my grandfather. I was eight years old standing on a beach in Tonga. Tonight it seemed I could almost hear him whispering in my ear."

Jake was thinking, and everyone was quiet. Then, without any warning, his eyes lit up, and he raised his fist. He almost screamed, "Let's hear it for our class!" Jake let out a whoop that had to be Tongan, and the students joined in with wild applause. He raised his hands to quiet them. Then speaking quietly and in humble tones, he said, "You guys are the greatest! But what am I going to do with that box?" The entire class laughed. Once again he raised his hands and a hush quickly fell over the crowd.

Cheyenne stood up and walked over to where Jake was standing. There were whispers throughout the class. Cheyenne assumed control and said, "Jake, would you stand right over there by that table?" Cheyenne smiled at him and said quietly so only he could hear, "It's my turn now."

Cheyenne turned to the class and Jake. "Since I am the teacher's assistant, a volunteer job, for which, by the way, I didn't volunteer, it has fallen on me to thank the man who made all of this possible, Brother Wolfgramm." Everyone in the class stood and clapped and chanted, "Jake! Jake! Jake!"

"To honor you, we wanted to buy you a really expensive present, but alas we spent all of our funds for you-know-what. So we thought and thought. We even tried to bribe a couple of girls at the U to take you on a date, but they declined as soon as we told them your name."

Everyone was hooting, cheering, and adding their own comments as Cheyenne continued. "So what we finally decided to give you was *us*. Now we know that's not much, but it's all we got. So you're stuck with us."

Cheyenne continued. "By 'us' I mean that we have a scrapbook of the big box and the small part that each of us played in the saga. Jenny, do you have the book? Would you come up here and present the book to the chief and tell him a little of what you have put in it."

Jenny went up to the front of the room carrying a huge oversized scrapbook. She said, "We had to have a book to match the box, so we found the biggest scrapbook that has ever been made, we think. Inside is a personal letter from each of us as well as many photos."

Craig called out, "It ain't much, Jake, but it's all we've got."

Cheyenne had one more thing to do, but Jake interrupted and said, "Thanks! That calls for another Haka." Jake assumed the stance and started the Tongan dance. It took about five minutes before Cheyenne regained control. "Jake, we have one more thing. You see, we have heard the story in roundabout ways of you and your grandfather and your coming to America. It took some work, but we were able to get word to your grandfather. We sent him copies of all of our letters to tell him how much you have meant to us. We asked him to write a letter back to you. We have that letter to read to you tonight. In fact, your father is going to read the it. Mr. Wolfgramm, will you come up here?"

To Jake's surprise, his father, Daniel Wolfgramm, walked to the front of the room and said in broken English, "Jake's grandfather is a man of dreams. He is respected by all his people. He told Jake many things when we left Tonga. He is very old now, but we will never forget him. This letter was written to Jacob by his grandfather, but he wanted all of you to hear it as well." He read the letter.

> *I have read the letters sent to me by Jacob's students. I am proud of my grandson. I also want to thank each of his students for being so kind to an old man and writing me letters. I am glad of the things that you have written to me of my grandson. Thank you.*
>
> *Jacob, sixteen years ago I watched you leave Tonga to go to America. I told you then that you had things to do in America. I knew it was so.*
>
> *Your students have asked me to write a letter to you because of the wonderful things you have done for them. Jacob, I told you then that there were things to do that only you could do. I still dream about you and I know that many people will thank you for helping them find their way through life.*
>
> *Jacob, the Lord will bless you always if you remember and never forget your gifts come from the Lord and were given to you to be used for his purposes. Though you have been blessed by the Lord, never forget who you are and where you came from. Never!*

Jacob, we are your people. You carry our star.
These things I write as a witness that they are true.
I know! I love you, Jacob Wolfgramm.

Joseph Wolfgramm

Cheyenne stood and said, "We just wanted you to know how much we care about you and how lucky we are to have a teacher who cares about us."

Everyone stood and cheered and again shouted, "Jake, Jake, Jake!"

Cheyenne sat back down in silence. Thoughts were swirling through her mind. So many dreams, so many fears, so much left behind, so much of life to live. Then she looked up, and there was her mother with outstretched arms.

Cheyenne got up and hugged her. "There is so much I want to tell you, Mom. My heart is so full."

"I want to hear every word. We have the whole Christmas holiday just to ourselves."

"Well, that's not entirely correct because . . . well . . . you see . . . I . . . I . . . may be spending some time with the GQ guy. I'll let you know, okay?" Cheyenne said with a twinkle in her eye.

Nichole looked surprised and excited and replied, "You mean the same guy you wouldn't even let drive you home from school?"

They both laughed and Cheyenne added, "It's a good thing I didn't have any money in the bank that day, isn't it?"

Jake stood up on the table and quieted the crowd. Cheyenne walked with her Mom and Richard over to the corner of the room. It was quieter there.

Harrison followed them and stood by her side. He put his arm around her and squeezed. Suddenly it was so quiet that Cheyenne could almost hear the falling snow—that is, between the thunderous beating of her heart.

Jake finally stood and said, "My grandfather is a very special person to me. I have not spoken with him for many years. This letter is a treasure that I will always keep. I thank you guys for caring."

After a moment, he continued. "Now all you kids better get home before Santa finds your bed empty. He might just pass you by, and we wouldn't want that to happen."

Craig stood up and said, "If he does we're gonna come lookin' for you, Jake!"

Everyone laughed.

They started filing out to their cars. Jake stood by the door and hugged all of his kids as they left that night. Cheyenne was the last to leave, with Harrison by her side.

Jake grabbed her in a bear hug. Finally, he let her go. Cheyenne kissed him on the cheek. "Jake, it's people like you who gave a person like me a chance. How can I ever pay you back for that?"

Jake looked into her eyes, smiled, and said, "You've already paid me back. All I have to do is look at Nichole. She has never been so happy, and it's all because of you, Cheyenne."

Jake turned to Harrison and asked, "And you, have you decided where you're going to play football next year?"

"I don't know," Harrison grinned, and with a twinkle in his eye, he added, "Cheyenne hasn't told me yet."

Epilogue

Well, that's Jake's story, or his students' story. Having been there on that Christmas Eve, he had felt what they had felt, and he would never trade one minute of it for anything. They were his misfits, his underprivileged "flakes." He would never forget them or that Christmas Eve.

Harrison went to Stanford and played football. He's now a physician practicing in Utah County.

Cheyenne went to the University of Utah and graduated with honors. She teaches seminary part time to high school seniors and is raising her family—three girls and a boy—with her high school sweetheart, a guy named Harrison.

Nichole doesn't miss a minute of her grandchildren's lives. The oldest is a girl who shares her name. Her grandson's nickname is GQ.

Jake kept the box around for years. He just didn't have the heart to toss the old thing out.

Early that fabled Christmas morning, Nichole and Richard sat on the couch in each other's arms. Cheyenne sat in the middle of the floor. She was surrounded by piles of wrapping paper that had been torn from packages and scattered across the room. The gifts were neatly stacked behind her—more gifts than she could imagine. "I told you he would spoil you," Nichole said. "He always told me that Christmas was for kids."

"Well, I certainly got more than I deserved. What about you?"

At that minute, the front door opened and a man and woman walked in without knocking. Cheyenne recognized the man immediately, and her eyes widened with fear. Nichole jumped up and threw her arms around the man, giving him a big hug. "Dad," she exclaimed, "I've missed you. I didn't know you would be back today!"

Cheyenne, who had thought of hiding under the wrapping paper, was stunned. Nichole hugged her mother and invited the visitors to sit down.

Father? But that doesn't make any sense! Cheyenne thought.

Nichole's father shook Richard's hand, sat down on the couch, and looked around the room until his eyes stopped on Cheyenne. He smiled. Cheyenne thought her heart was going to stop.

"You look surprised, Cheyenne," he said.

Cheyenne tried to answer, but nothing would come. Nichole sat down next to Cheyenne and put her arm around her. "I've never told her," she said to her father.

Her father smiled and said, "We decided to come home early so we could be here for Christmas. Besides, it was me who told Nichole that you don't have to throw something away just because it's broken. I think I forgot."

"Cheyenne," he continued, "I've been a judge for many years. I have seen a lot of teenagers come through my court. When I allowed my daughter to take you home, it was against my better judgment. She has always been extremely headstrong, and I didn't think she knew what she was doing. Nor did I think you had a chance to make something of yourself. Maybe I'm not as smart as I think I am.

"I've followed your progress. Nichole has spoken to me almost every day. I am here to tell you that I was dead wrong. Apparently, Cheyenne, you are one of those rare people we call a survivor. You have become a beautiful young woman whom I almost didn't recognize. From what I've been told, you're a wonderful person as well. It's fitting that today is Christmas and that we celebrate the Lord who gave His life for each of us. He also suffered for us all that we might be forgiven of our shortcomings and be able to live with him again.

"There is something I want to give you today, Cheyenne, which is also a gift to Nichole and Richard. Tomorrow, I am going to sign the final adoption decree, and I will seal and expunge all of your juvenile records. It is as the Lord said, 'Your sins are forgiven and I remember them no more.' This also means that as of now, you have a mother and father to report to, and I know for a fact that you have made them very happy. They love you more than you will ever know."

Cheyenne was stunned and silent. Thoughts swirled in her mind. It was too much to comprehend, and she was overwhelmed—so many dreams and fears, so much left behind, and so much of life to live.

Cheyenne was indeed Judge Wentworth's granddaughter.

Author's Note

Most of the characters in this story are fictional, although some personalities are based on actual people. The events portrayed in the story, however, are based upon events that occurred at Granite High School in 1989.

The teller of this story was none other than Molonai Hola. He knows the story because he was there. Jacob Wolfgramm was actually Molonai (Nai to his friends) Hola. He taught seminary at Granite High School in 1989 while playing football at the University of Utah and serving as president of the university student body.

Nai eventually graduated from the University of Utah. Thereafter, he earned a master's of business administration from Arizona State University, a master's degree from Thunderbird International School of Business, and finally an executive master's degree from Harvard in business. He really did come from a dirt floor in Tonga to graduate from the most elite university in the world, and his grandfather in Tonga did make many of the predictions set forth in this story, although I'm not sure Nai's accomplishments are related to his grandfather's predictions or because someone told him he couldn't do it.

In 2003 Nai ran for mayor of Salt Lake City. He lost but finished a strong third. A few of his friends question it, but Nai and politics probably aren't finished.

Dennis L. Mangrum has practiced law for more than thirty years in California and Utah. Before law school, he was a civil engineer, having graduated with a master's degree from the University of Utah while competing in football and wrestling. Earlier, he graduated from West High School in Salt Lake City and was named all-state in both football and wrestling. There he learned about life, working hard, and never giving up. The unstated school motto at the time was that if you didn't beat them during the game, you would after the game.

Dennis has always loved to write despite his English teachers' opinions regarding his ability. He self-published his first novel several years ago. It sits in boxes in his basement. After that debacle, he decided to take a writing class in which he learned the basic rudiments of writing a novel. *Seasons of Salvation* is his first published novel, and he thanks Cedar Fort for giving him the chance.

Dennis fancies himself, first, a baseball coach (having coached at Brighton High in one capacity or another for more than fifteen years); second, a writer; and third, an attorney, a job that allows him to support his other more important habits. His wife fancies him a husband and tells him to write on his own time, which means after everything else is done and everyone is in bed.

He lives with his wife and high school sweetheart, Elizabeth (Ence) Mangrum, in Sandy, Utah. They are the parents of three children still at home and four married and on their own.